NIGHT RAID

It was full dark when Kendrick took up his position by the rain barrel at the corner of the cabin. A half hour passed, and he heard a thin clink of metal as a shod hoof struck a bit of rock.

He waited until they were within twenty feet; then he blasted away with his six-gun, fanning it empty while the rifle still lay across his lap. Both men went down. A single shot came hammering into the logs above Kendrick's head.

The gun slammed again, and Kendrick replied, using the rifle to aim at the orange flash. He was aware that riders were moving across the valley toward the scene. The drumming hoofbeats came close. The enemy was moving in . . .

Also by E. E. Halleran
Published by Ballantine Books:

SHADOW OF THE BIG HORN

DEVIL'S CANYON

CIMARRON THUNDER

SPANISH RIDGE

BY

E. E. HALLERAN

BALLANTINE BOOKS • NEW YORK

Library of Congress Catalog Card Number: 57-12240

ISBN 0-345-29436-X

Manufactured in the United States of America

First Edition: February 1957
Second Printing: March 1981

1

SINCE the first pink streaks of dawn had cut the eastern gloom Crook's troopers had been pushing northward through country that was alternately grassy and bleak, the ordered blue ranks ominously silent. Dusty, be-whiskered riders knew that this was not just another day of weary travel. The Crow and Shoshone scouts had gone out before daylight. The supply train had been left be-hind under a strong guard of the Fourth Infantry. Two hundred foot-sloggers of the Ninth had been mounted on supply mules to reinforce the cavalry units. No bugles were sounding, all orders being passed by word of mouth. Even the greenest recruit could read that kind of sign.

A little before eight o'clock the column broke out of the canyon country into a grassy valley where a sluggish stream lazed along between thickets of wild roses. Orders came back along the line and the advance split, half of the little army fording the stream. The routine maneuver was smartly executed and within a few minutes the entire force was strung out along either bank of the creek, mounted infantry and two battalions of the Third Cavalry on the left bank while the Second Cavalry and a battalion of the Third remained on the right bank. Then the order came to halt and unsaddle, only a thin picket line being thrown out.

To the men of Troop L, heading the advance of the Third, it seemed like a dangerous order. Only a little dis-tance away the valley closed up into a dark canyon, high bluffs closing in from the northwest to form barriers on two sides. Any number of hostiles might be lurking there within striking distance of the bivouac.

Sergeant Cavanagh, L's newest platoon sergeant, rode back along the line, his voice a little pompous as he or-dered, "Keep your weapons and equipment ready, men.

5

We'll rest the horses all we can while we wait to hear from the scouts."

Trooper Michaels of the first squad grinned at his companions as Cavanagh rode away. "Ed's gettin' real important with that extra stripe on his arm," he observed. "Made it sound like restin' the horses was his own pet idea."

"No idea to brag about," Private Hooper grumbled. "We'll be in a devil of a fix if them Sioux bust outa the brush now."

Corporal Kendrick looked around from inspecting the bivouac. "If we're jumped we'll dismount and fight on foot anyway. Just make sure your carbine's cleaner than your neck, Hooper."

There was a general laugh in which the burly Hooper joined. In the three dreary weeks since the column had left Fort Fetterman no one had done much washing. The regiment was dirty, and a little proud of it.

"Hoop's nervous, Corporal," Michaels declared. "These green rookies get awful proddy when they smell hostiles—or maybe when they know the hostiles can smell *them*."

Another laugh broke out. Hooper was a bearded veteran in his third enlistment while Michaels was barely eighteen, his pink complexion making him appear even younger. Kendrick chuckled as Hooper swore disgustedly. At a time like this jokes did no harm.

The squadron sprawled out as comfortably as possible, the men picking grassy spots where the sweetbriars were not too thick and keeping up the banter they used to conceal a growing apprehension. Ever since that Sioux sniping attack on Tongue River it had been clear to all that a fight was coming up. A strong force of hostiles was in front of the army and the Indian commander was Crazy Horse himself. That was enough to make veterans careful.

Sergeant Cavanagh came back after a few minutes, staring sourly at the troopers on the ground. "Keep those men awake, Corporal!" he snapped. "We may have to move in a hurry when the scouts come in with their reports."

"We'll be ready," Kendrick assured him, not bothering to look up.

"Be sure of that!" Cavanagh ordered testily. "You're not out of the army yet, you know."

Kendrick rolled over to stare up at the man in the saddle. "You think you need to tell me my duty, Ed?" he asked, still lazily quiet. There was a striking resemblance between the man in the saddle and the one on the ground. Each was just under six feet, lean and saddle-tough from much campaigning. Each wore a mustache which was now just a particularly brushy part of a full beard. Neither had shaved since leaving Fort Fetterman.

Cavanagh glowered but relaxed a little. "No hard feelings, Tom," he said in an altered tone. "I'm just passing the orders."

Young Michaels offered another comment as the lanky sergeant rode away. "Maybe Hoop ain't the only nervous jigger around here. Sounds to me like our new sarge has got some jiggles in his stomach too."

"Cavanagh was fighting Indians while you were still wearing diapers," Kendrick told him. "Don't be blackguarding your betters."

Michaels was not disturbed by the reprimand. "I reckon he ain't really scared. Just nervous about that extra stripe. Maybe he knows it oughta be on your sleeve instead of on his."

"That's not your worry," Kendrick told him shortly. "And it's not mine. In another month I'll be a sod-buster. Cavanagh's staying in; he can use the extra stripe."

"If either of you live the month out," Hooper added grimly.

A little man who had not said a word since dismounting suddenly spoke. He was lying flat on his back and staring into the bright blue of the June sky but the words came sonorously, as though delivered from a platform. "Methinks friend Hooper doth apprehend more than cool reason comprehends."

Hooper snorted. "More damn Shakespeare quotin', I suppose!"

The little man did not change his position. "In a way. I took certain liberties with *Midsummer Night's Dream*."

7

"Meanin' what?"

"Meaning you shouldn't holler before you're hurt."

"I'm hurt enough already," Hooper retorted. "We broiled on the South Cheyenne, froze on Wind Creek, baked again on the Powder—and now we're waitin' for Crazy Horse to start shootin'. This blasted expedition was jinxed from the start."

The little man rolled over to wink at Kendrick. "I quote again," he said solemnly. "The slings and arrows of outrageous misfortune doth make cowards of us all."

Kendrick laughed. "And makes us garble our quotations," he added. "I've been reading some of your books and I happen to remember a part of that one."

"Takes genius to put two quotations together," the little trooper said calmly. "And don't be so picky; these chumps won't know the difference if I form a partnership between Hamlet and whoever it was I swiped the other phrase from."

Kendrick let the talk run on, content to bask in the warm June sunshine. Usually he was amused by Trooper Smith's tongue-in-cheek culture but today he was in no mood for it. His own affairs were too heavy on his mind. That last letter from his Uncle Bill had sounded ominous, hinting that it would be well for Tom to get home as soon as possible. The letter had arrived on the same day as the marching orders and Kendrick had been getting farther away from Uncle Bill every day.

Nor was that all. A strong force of hostiles was in the vicinity, a force which would be desperate and in no mood to retreat. The Sioux scouts must know that three armies were closing in on them, Gibbon coming down from Fort Ellis, Terry and Custer marching west from Fort Abraham Lincoln, and Crook driving up from the Platte. The Sioux chiefs would have to fight—and Crazy Horse was just the leader to do it, particularly since his own village was supposed to be directly in the line of Crook's march. Crook was due for trouble.

"It ain't goot," Trooper Meinecke growled in a strong German accent. "Der signs are pat. Wrong date. In March it vas der seventeenth ven Crazy Horse cuts us up in der snow."

Trooper Smith had a comment—and a broad wink toward Kendrick. "That was the unlucky Ides of March, Hans," he explained solemnly. "Known in Ulster as St. Patrick's Day. In June that number is not unlucky. Some of our boys won a battle on Bunker Hill on June seventeenth."

Kendrick grinned, realizing that seventeen was also a number for him to remember. He would be out of the army on July seventeenth. Then his grin faded as a crackle of gunfire drifted down from the ragged bluffs to the north. He jumped to his feet, making sure that every man was awake.

"Get ready to move," he ordered. "Either those crazy Shoshones have gone on another buffalo hunt or they've run afoul of the hostiles."

Even as he spoke he knew it was the latter. Gunfire was coming from two widely spaced quarters. Two parties were doing the shooting, probably at each other. Buffalo didn't shoot back.

The men of the first squad were standing to horse when Sergeant Cavanagh began to bellow orders. A dozen Crow and Shoshone scouts had appeared on the north bluff, evidently in full retreat before an unseen enemy.

Saddles were cinched on in a hurry and before the Indian scouts could get down into the valley the Second Battalion was formed into line while the infantry moved out afoot to form a skirmish line at the base of the bluffs.

"Devil of a place to fight Indians," Cavanagh growled as he pulled up beside Kendrick. "They got us in a pocket. We should have formed on the bluffs."

Kendrick nodded without speaking and after a moment Cavanagh went on, "Don't think I'm getting rank-happy because I got this stripe, Tom. Captain Vroom thinks the same way. Looks like we'll have to gun our way out if the hostiles are as strong as the scouts think."

Again Kendrick merely nodded. He and Ed Cavanagh had served together for nearly ten years, riding patrols against the southern tribes along the Santa Fe Trail and more recently campaigning against the Sioux and Cheyennes in Wyoming. They had been close without ever

9

becoming real friends but they understood each other. Now it seemed natural that they should meet danger together.

Cavanagh seemed to feel it most. He kept the silence for a full minute but then went on, "I didn't mean anything by that crack a while ago, Tom. A bit jealous, maybe. Right now I can envy a man who's getting out of the army."

"Your time is up the same week as mine."

"Sure. But I've got no place to go. While you played it smart with that homestead claim I was playing poker at Amos Trappe's place. It makes a difference."

A staff lieutenant galloped up with orders and Cavanagh hustled away. By that time the friendly scouts were running through the valley in wild confusion, other panic-stricken Indians following them down from the bluffs. Officers herded them back through the grim ranks while non-coms steadied their men against the threat of general panic. As had been predicted by many veterans, the Crows and Shoshones were not proving very sturdy in the face of opposition. Having feared the Sioux for so many generations they could not believe that their white allies were strong enough for any safety.

Kendrick heard a civilian scout reporting that the hostiles were indeed numerous but by that time he could see the enemy for himself. Perhaps a hundred mounted warriors had appeared on the bluffs a half mile away, most of them making derisive motions toward the white troopers while others knelt to blaze away with long-range rifle fire.

A bugle blared its urgent demand from the right bank of the stream and the waiting men of Troop L could see Colonel Mills's battalion moving in across their right flank. Mills was going to charge the bluffs where the Sioux were putting on their show.

Then Captain Vroom and his lieutenants began to shout orders and a second bugle pealed orders from behind the Third's line. Troops B, D, F, and L were to swing left behind the infantry and charge the bluffs on the western perimeter of the valley. There a second strong

10

force of Sioux had appeared and was threatening the ammunition train.

Kendrick watched his squad carefully as the bugle sang again, seeing that each man wheeled his horse with the proper precision. Steadiness now could mean a great deal. He snapped a couple of sharp commands and then they were riding hard at the steep slope which flanked the sweetbriars on the western side. Weary horses responded well and the four units went into the climb, a storm of gunfire breaking over and around them as the swarming Sioux opened fire from the summit.

A man dropped on Kendrick's right. In the next squad a horse went down, its rider scrambling to his feet and opening fire on the Indians with his carbine as comrades swept past him. Firing was general now, the Sioux having commenced long-range firing from ridges on three sides of the valley.

It was bloody work at the crest of the ridge but the Second Battalion pressed home the charge without faltering, driving the Indians from their positions with revolvers. A few men moved to pursue the retreating foe but the bugle sounded again and they pulled back into line. New orders rang out and the men dismounted, leaving horse holders to keep the animals below the rocky crest where they would be out of the line of enemy fire.

In the interval while the dismounted skirmish line waited for orders Kendrick took account of his squad. Trooper Michaels was the only one missing. He had been the man who had gone down first. Otherwise there were no casualties in the squad. The attack had been a success. The Second Battalion held the west side while Mills's force was holding firm on the northern bluff nearest to the gorge. Other troops were driving the Sioux from a ridge farther south while the reserves in the valley held their positions unneeded.

"Out of der pocket anyvay," Trooper Meinecke growled on Kendrick's left. "Now vot happens?"

"Looks like it'll be up to the Sioux," Kendrick replied. "They seem to be running the show."

Sergeant Cavanagh stamped nervously along the line, a carbine clutched in a lean brown hand. "What do you

11

make of it, Tom?" he asked in a low voice. "Sioux don't attack like that unless they've got something on their mean minds. Think they're trying to suck us into an ambush?"

"Could be. They've done it before." He pointed to another line of bluffs some three hundred yards beyond. "Take a good squint at those devils, Ed. I don't believe they're Sioux; they look like Cheyennes to me."

Cavanagh nodded and hurried away to speak urgently to Captain Vroom. Kendrick smiled thinly. That was Cavanagh's pet trick. Probably it had helped to get him his stripes. Not that it made any difference, the scouts having already reported Cheyennes with the Sioux, but it was typical of Cavanagh to be alert to every opportunity for making himself look good.

The Cheyennes on the second crest began to demonstrate wildly again, riding their ponies madly along the ragged heights and firing random shots at the waiting troopers. It was clearly the old Indian trick of inviting pursuit for ambush purposes but word came that a second attack was to be made. No units were to advance beyond the second line of bluffs, however; General Crook was not to be fooled by such an ancient strategem.

The horseholders came up then and the cavalrymen swung into their saddles at the command, shoving carbines into saddleboots. Such weapons could not be used effectively from a running horse so this was to be a pistol fight. Indians seemed to fear the six-shooter almost as much as they scorned the carbine and the saber. Partly for that reason Crook's men had left their sabers at Fort Fetterman.

Voice and bugle commands rang again and the blue line moved forward across the rocky ground between the ridges. This time the Sioux retreated with only a small show of resistance. A cheer broke out at the easy victory but then the men were on the heights and could see that a third line of low cliffs confronted them. Now the Indian strategy was clear.

"Take cover and wait," the order came. Once more tired horses were pulled back behind the rocks and the dusty blue line bellied down in a glum sort of silence. Men didn't like what they were seeing.

Cavanagh came along after a few minutes of delay, his lips tight as he glanced down at Kendrick. "Think they're trying to work a Fetterman on us, Tom?" he asked.

"Maybe. They could have a thousand warriors hidden back in those crags. It could get real nasty."

"Take care of yourself, fella. You've got places to go."

It was the nearest thing to sentiment Kendrick had ever heard from Cavanagh and he stared for a moment before commenting, "Maybe you could do the same. Amos Trappe needs a partner in that new trading post of his. Uncle Bill says he's doing good."

"So I heard," Cavanagh nodded. "Got a deal with Floyd Mitchell. You remember him?"

"Can't say that I do. Army man?"

"In a way. Kind of a gun slick. Ran beef contracts for the army down that way. Him and Amos ought to make a good pair—if they don't kill each other. Neither one'll dare turn his back, that's sure."

He hurried away as though unwilling to continue the conversation and Kendrick was left to ponder. Somehow he had never understood Ed Cavanagh.

A half hour passed, the Sioux and Cheyennes continuing their aggravation tactics but on a somewhat reduced scale. Meanwhile three battalions of the Third held the second line of bluffs, the Indian scouts and the reserves still back in the valley of the Rosebud.

Then heavy firing broke out somewhere to the right of Kendrick's position and word came along that the fight was between Indians. Some of the Crows had moved up beyond the infantry units and had been attacked by the Sioux under Crazy Horse himself. L's troopers could see none of the action but the rattle of gunfire suggested a brisk skirmish.

"About time those Crows did something besides eat," Trooper Smith commented. "I was beginning to think they wouldn't stand up to a Sioux at all."

"Maybe they'll do all right. They've got plenty of reason to hate the Sioux."

"And plenty of reason to be scared to death of 'em," Smith retorted. "That's what I don't like. As the bard puts it, 'Our fears do make us traitors'."

Kendrick chuckled. "I'll give you another. 'Yet death we fear. That makes these odds all even.' I think that comes from *Measure for Measure*."

The little trooper shook his head. "I should never have let you read my books. Hoist with me own petard."

Trumpeting on the right indicated some sort of help being sent to the Crow allies and presently cheering indicated that the Sioux assault had been beaten off. It seemed to be the signal for the Cheyennes in front of L to redouble their efforts. A few snipers began to work forward among the rocks where they could reach the cavalry position with rifle fire, their mounted companions keeping up a wild show as though daring the troopers to come after them.

"Looks like we'll have to oblige them," Kendrick growled. "Their rifles out-range us and if enough of them get among the rocks they'll have us pinned down."

"Suits me," Hooper rumbled. "We got a score to settle for poor Michaels."

"Forget it!" Kendrick ordered. "You can't afford to lose your head when you're fighting Indians."

Ten minutes later the expected order arrived. The Second Battalion was to clear the Indians from in front of the entire left wing of the army's position.

2

FOR the third time the disciplined routine of the charge was performed but this time Kendrick found himself thinking briefly of irrelevant matters. How so many different men could drop their personalities at a bugle call and become mere cogs in a machine. The grumbling Hooper, the scholarly but vaguely picaresque Smith, the dour and gloomy Meinecke, the conniving Cavanagh— and even a somewhat frustrated fellow named Kendrick. For the moment their thoughts were not their own. For the moment they could only ride hard at a line of chalky

14

bluffs where a lot of Cheyennes were making crazy motions.

The impression passed in less time than he would have needed to explain it and he was again the veteran non-com, keeping an eye on his men even as he did his fair share of the fighting. This time the Indians did not run so quickly and there was a brisk fight at the crest of the rise, both sides suffering casualties. Then the Cheyennes began to retreat slowly, fighting as they went back.

For a few minutes there was no pursuit, the white commanders a little suspicious of this change in tactics on the part of the enemy. The terrain was different now. This third ridge did not overlook another shallow valley but simply leveled off into an expanse of broken rocks, washed gullies and freak clay formations which reminded Kendrick of some of the badlands they had traversed back in Wyoming. Apparently the Indians proposed to use this ragged country to make a fighting retreat, always holding sniping positions a little ahead of the army's advance.

"Forward!" the order came again. "Close formation. Beat them out of those rocks!" It was the only sensible thing to do; the troops could not hold the rim while the enemy was in position to harass their lines with rifle fire.

The cavalrymen plunged forward, immediately exchanging shots with the skulking Indians, and the entire line soon found itself engaged in a series of swirling fights where squads became the only recognizable units. The advance was no longer a charge but a dogged push, some squads making more headway than others so that the line ceased to exist.

Kendrick tried to keep his men in some sort of order but after the first few minutes he could not tell where the rest of L was. A few Cheyennes had slipped through the line and there was fighting on all sides. Still they seemed to be pushing the Indians back and he hoped that other squads were doing the same thing. Certainly there had been no trumpeted orders to cease the advance.

Suddenly the order was not necessary. The first squad found itself in a sort of pocket with fire coming from all sides. A bullet singed Kendrick's upper arm but he killed the Cheyenne who had fired the shot, turning his revolver then on another brown form that had popped up out of some brush to aim a rifle at Meinecke. For a good five minutes a miniature but deadly battle raged there among the rocks and bushes, casualties about even on both sides. Kendrick knew that Hooper and three other men were down, apparently dead, and he felt sure that at least five Indians had been killed. If this was the trap they had anticipated it was a good one.

Then heavier fire began to come from the top of a chalky butte and he yelled for his men to pull back and take cover. He wheeled his horse as he shouted the command, a numbing pain striking at his thigh as he did so. Somewhere to his left a man screamed in agony and far to the rear a bugle sounded recall. The note seemed thin and dangerously far away.

Smith and Meinecke were the only ones with him as he drove his mount for the cover of a ledge, Smith shouting a quick warning. There were Indians in the line of retreat.

"Dismount!" Kendrick yelled. "Take cover. We'll have to hold them until the rest of our outfit closes up."

He swung from the saddle with the words, falling heavily as his right leg failed to hold his weight. Slugs were chipping the chalky rocks all around him, coming from three sides now, but he pulled himself up by a stirrup, hopping on his left leg to try for a split in a nearby rock. The move took him out of the worst fire but there were three Indians bearing down on them now, moving in from what had once been his rear. Two of the Cheyennes fired as he spotted them and he could feel his horse slump against him. He sprang clear, falling into the hole he had been trying to reach. His senses reeled from the fall and from his wounds but he pulled himself together long enough to cut down one of the charging savages. Trooper Meinecke killed the other one, cursing in German as he did so. Then Kendrick knew no more.

Returning consciousness was a confused sort of business. The first sensation he knew was one of pain, a pain that refused to localize itself but which seemed to be one big ache all over his body. Then his impressions began

16

to sort themselves out. He smelled horse sweat . . . and blood. He heard distant gunshots. He felt a numbing weight on his right forearm. There was a cramp in his back.

Finally it worked out in an understandable pattern. He was in the little cleft of rocks which had seemed like a good emergency shelter, pinned there and almost covered by the body of his own dead horse. Evidently the horse had fallen against him just as Meinecke killed that charging Cheyenne.

He listened for sounds of movement nearby. There was none. The battle must have swept beyond this particular bit of territory. But why hadn't Meinecke or Smith come to his aid?

The answer to that seemed grimly certain so he refused to think more about it. He found that he could use his left arm without too much pain so he braced himself with it, heaving against the inert flesh of the fallen horse and dragging the pinned right arm clear. That done he could raise himself and look out over the dead animal. Meinecke's body was out there. Scalped. The dead Cheyennes had been taken away.

That told him something. Evidently Meinecke had killed the only Indians who knew that a trooper had fallen into the crevice behind the dead horse. Other Indians had come up in time to kill the German but not in time to realize that another soldier was close by. Kendrick decided that he had been lucky to have been knocked unconscious. Only his utter silence had saved him from the scalpers who had ravaged the little battlefield.

He tried to estimate the state of the main fight from the sounds of firing and was surprised to see that a fair portion of the third plateau was visible from his hiding place. He could see the smoke of a brisk fight to the north but eastward toward the valley there was no activity. He glimpsed a few Indians firing from behind cover and the sight was not cheering. He was well behind the Indian lines; the troops had pulled back.

When he slumped back into the hole he became conscious of the pain in his right thigh. A clumsy examination

17

told him that he had lost a lot of blood but he could move the leg, so the bullet had not broken any bones. Using his jackknife as best he could in the cramped quarters, he slit the trousers around the blood-soaked area, hacking off a piece of his shirt tail as a pad and binding it into place with his neckerchief. The smaller wound on his upper arm did not seem to be bleeding much so he let it alone.

He rested for a few minutes after the effort, trying to get the shakes out of his fingers. He was annoyed at himself that he should tremble so much. He knew it was shock rather than fear but still he didn't like the idea. A ten-year veteran wasn't supposed to get shaky.

After a while he began to grope for his revolver but could not locate it. As nearly as he could remember he had been aiming it at one of the Cheyennes when the horse fell on him. Probably the gun was under the horse near where his right hand had been pinned. Without help he couldn't hope to get it. Digging was out of the question; there was only bare rock beneath the dead animal.

He pulled his good left leg under him and raised up as far as the overhanging rock would permit. He wanted to survey his chances for getting clear of the trap into which he had fallen. The dead horse had saved him but it had also bottled him up completely. Even with two good arms and legs he couldn't have moved the dead beast without help.

He could see out across the horse's barrel but the opening was only large enough to look through. His shoulders would not go. However, he did see that his carbine was still in its scabbard, either overlooked or unwanted by the Indians.

By twisting his body a little he managed to get his right arm through the opening, groping for the butt of the carbine. His finger tips reached the stock but he couldn't get a grip that would let him slide the weapon from its sheath. After straining for several minutes without results he had to slump back into the hole and rest. The shakes came back. Even in good condition it would have been almost impossible for him to get enough finger tip pressure on that smooth stock to permit him to slip the weapon

18

out; certainly he could not hope to get results when weakness was tearing at him.

He had to do some thinking. One possibility was obvious. He unbuttoned his galluses after first removing the heavy cartridge belt. It was no great trick to make a slip knot in the suspenders and seconds later he was shoving his right hand through the opening to dangle the crude noose toward the carbine butt. Fortunately the gun was not pressed hard against the body of the horse and in a moment he knew that the loop had slipped into place. When he tightened on it he could feel the carbine move a little.

Careful maneuvering brought the gun up far enough so that he could hook a finger into the trigger guard. The rest was easy. There was scant room in the hole for handling the carbine but fortunately the Springfield was a stubby gun and he managed to load it and make it ready for use. Then he felt a little better. With forty-eight of the original sixty cartridges still in his belt he could feel a little less helpless.

His upper arm was bleeding from the way he had been forcing it against the overhanging rock while he worked so he eased back, clamping his right hand over the wound to stop the blood. The enforced rest let him recover a measure of strength. He pulled himself up. There was no power in his left leg and the pain was still intense but he felt that all bleeding had ceased. With a little more rest he might be able to make an attempt at reaching the army's lines—if he could get the dead horse out of the way.

There was a bitter irony in the thought. For months he had been looking forward to the end of his enlistment, anxious to get away from the army and back to the spot where his ambitions had been so long delayed by his own bad judgment. Now he suddenly had reversed his thinking. Getting back to the army was much more vital than getting away from it.

He turned to the problem at hand. He had a notion that he might move the dead horse a little by using the carbine as a lever. However, he did not propose to commit himself to the effort until he knew a little more about

19

the situation on the battlefield. For the present he was well hidden if not comfortable.

The fighting had dwindled appreciably. The time ought to be well past noon, Kendrick decided, noting that the shadows were still short but swinging a little with the sun. The heat was intense, its shimmering waves making the gray and yellow rocks seem unreal.

He tried to guess what the Indians were doing but the desultory firing told him little. He thought the troops must still be holding the line of bluffs at the edge of the ragged plateau but it seemed likely that neither side had made any serious move since the charge which had brought disaster to Troop L; at least, he assumed that other squads of L had been cut off along with his own.

He watched for a good hour, his cramped position the worst part of the situation. The leg was not bothering him too much now but he had constant kinks in sound muscles. Twice small bands of warriors passed close to his hiding place. The Cheyennes were getting restless. Something big seemed to be building. Maybe it would involve an attack that would rescue him.

The first sound of combat came from far to the north. A distant bugle sounded Boots and Saddles. Somebody was ready to move. Maybe Colonel Mills would hit the northern front and try to roll back the Indian line.

He waited for the stirring clamor of the Charge but nothing happened. A cavalry unit had been ordered into the saddle but was not attacking. What did it mean?

Then he noted a stir of movement among the Indians within his range of vision. Warriors were beginning to move to the left, toward the area where those trumpets had blared. The Cheyennes who had been harassing the Second Battalion with their rifle fire were moving to reinforce the Sioux on the northern angle. Either they anticipated an attack from Mills or they proposed to make some kind of attack as a result of his movement.

The hot silence became oppressive. None of the Indians were sniping now and there was an answering silence from the army positions. Kendrick didn't like the idea of it. When two strong forces had been slugging away at each other all day in a bloody stalemate it was ominous

20

for such a silence to develop. He had heard old-timers talk about the lull which preceded Pickett's charge at Gettysburg.

The silence lasted several minutes and then the dull crackle of carbine fire resumed. The soldiers along the skirmish line were firing. That did not sound good to the man in the hole. The Indians must be the ones preparing to attack. The troops were simply trying to hamper them with a casual fire. It was beginning to appear that General Crook's strike against the Sioux had turned into an all-out Sioux attack on Crook.

It seemed reasonable in the light of what had already happened. Crazy Horse must have met the blue column with sufficient force to make a real challenge. The wily chief had spent most of the day trying to lure the troops into such an ambush as had meant extermination to Captain Fetterman's command ten years earlier. When the ambush attempt failed Crazy Horse had brought up his reserves for a direct attack.

Still nothing big happened. An hour passed and Kendrick realized that the afternoon was waning. Still plenty of daylight for a fight but the wrong time of day for anything big to be developing. Unless both sides intended to continue long-range skirmishing during the night there would have to be some kind of assault pretty soon.

Then he heard it. A crackle of shots from the north swelled into a continuing roll of fire, even the faint shrieks of warriors drifting down on the warm air of the still afternoon. Those war whoops meant an Indian attack. Probably Crazy Horse had found a weakness in the blue line, maybe a hole left by whatever movement Mills's battalion had made. When the bugles began to blow in the upper valley of the Rosebud Kendrick could almost see what was happening. The Second Cavalry, held in reserve all day, was being hurled into the breach.

The battle swelled into a crescendo of angry sound, seeming to spill out along the line toward Kendrick as other units took it up. Kendrick saw dark forms in front of him running from rock to rock and he knew that the Sioux and Cheyennes were sniping all along the line, probably trying to find another weak point or at least to

21

keep Crook from sending any help to the main point of attack. Again Kendrick considered it an ominous sign. This was no longer the army's battle; it was being fought along the lines dictated by Crazy Horse.

He propped himself up as best he could, watching through the narrow gap between the dead horse and the rock overhang. Smoke and dust rolled up in the distance where the firing was heaviest, the spot where Mills had once held the line. It continued in that way for the better part of an hour but then he could sense that it was moving closer to him. Bugles sounded with increasing frequency and he knew that the army was again on the attack. The Sioux had been halted but the Indians were not retreating through the gap they had made; instead they were entangling the whole front in a skirmishing withdrawal.

A brisk fight broke out directly in front of him and through the pall of smoke and dust he could see both Sioux and Cheyennes. Once he saw two troopers but they disappeared quickly as though they had been the spearhead of an assault that had been beaten back. After that he saw that the Indians were really pulling back under cover of the smoke, leaving a few warriors to put up a show of belligerence. Finally the skirmishers retreated and the western perimeter of the valley was silent.

Dusk was falling now but he made no attempt to break out of his gruesome prison. The fighting had died away on all fronts but he couldn't be sure there were no Indians between himself and the army lines. Accordingly he waited. The safe course gave him more time to let the blood clot on his wounds before he began to exert himself.

He even slept a little, weariness stronger than discomfort. In his uneasy sleep he dreamed, waking to thoughts of his own mistakes. One wrong move had been responsible for his present position. He should never have reenlisted.

It was not a new thought. He had blamed himself many times for the error even though he knew that such second-guessing was a waste of time. Five years ago it had seemed reasonably certain that he would stay at Fort Union where he could continue to establish his homestead claim in his spare time. The army pay would help while he was getting the land to some sort of paying status. He could hardly have guessed that the army would promptly transfer him north. It was just one of those things. His only real mistake had been in assuming that the army would do the reasonable thing.

Once more he forced his mind back to the dreary present. Maybe there was still a chance that he would see New Mexico and Uncle Bill again. Certainly he wouldn't make it by fretting over old mistakes.

With darkness offering him a measure of protection he began the effort he knew must be made. Unloading the carbine for safety's sake, he wedged its barrel under the body of the horse, trying for leverage at an angle which might permit him to move the animal's hind quarters. The first real heave was rewarded with a full inch but after that he couldn't gain a bit. Five minutes of effort left him weak and spent so he rested again, listening to faint sounds of movement in the night.

There was a good chance that the movements were those of his own comrades but he didn't dare gamble on it. An outcry now might bring some of the Indians he had so far eluded.

Finally the sounds ceased and he still did not know whether he had been hearing friend or foe. It seemed clear that both sides had withdrawn from the area but there was no way for him to guess how far either had gone.

A second try at moving the horse proved vain. He collapsed into a cramped heap, falling asleep in spite of his aches and pains. When he awakened once more he could hear only the faint yapping of coyotes. Probably fighting over a corpse which had not been removed from the battlefield, he thought. He wondered how long it would be until some predator came to feed upon the horse which had become his jailor. While he was considering some of the unpleasant possibilities in that idea he slept again, fatigue and delayed shock too strong for even imagination to overcome.

3

DAWN was graying beyond the Rosebud's little valley when he awoke again, discovering that cramped muscles had made his legs almost useless. He could scarcely get the sound leg under him but he forced himself to the effort and was able to look out through the hole, making sure that no Indians remained in the vicinity. Then he began to work at the dead horse once more.

Painful effort gained him another inch and he found that he could almost get his shoulders through the opening. At the same time he realized another horrid possibility. When the day's heat began to affect the dead animal there would probably be some bloating. His position would become more dangerous as well as more nauseating.

Daylight was strengthening so he took time to study the position of the carcass. He had moved it a couple of inches but then it had stuck. Now he saw that it was probably the saddle that was causing the trouble. Either the saddle or some of its gear had become hooked on a bit of projecting rock. The jackknife came out again and he sawed through the cinch. The leather parted with an audible snap: the dead horse had already begun to bloat. He had to move fast.

Again the carbine became a lever but this time the results were quick. The carcass slid a good two inches now that the saddle was not acting as a catch. He heaved again and the opening was big enough. He went through head first, using his good hand to pull himself over far enough so that he could fall the rest of the way. After that he lay still for a few minutes, gathering his waning energies for the next move. He was free but he was still in plenty of trouble.

After he became steady again he looked to the carbine, cleaning its muzzle as best he could. He didn't think he

24

had injured the weapon so he dropped a shell into the breach and prepared to move. He knew that he must be several miles from the river valley but the only possible course was to head for it. He didn't dare force the use of his right leg so there was only one way to travel. He started crawling, dragging the wounded leg behind him.

He avoided the three ghastly corpses which the Indians had hacked so unmercifully but fifty yards toward the first ledge he found another dead trooper, a man from his own squad. It was a little soldier named Kirk and he was lying concealed by a clump of brush between jagged rocks. He had not been stripped or mutilated like the others. Kendrick dragged himself to the corpse and took the revolver which was still partly clasped in the dead fingers. A case like his own, he thought; Kirk had been killed by some Indian who did not survive to despoil his victim.

The six-shooter was empty but there were a half dozen cartridges remaining in the cartouche and another dozen in one of the dead man's pants pockets. Kendrick secured his prizes and crawled away.

He did another hundred yards and rested, worried about the way his hands and the good knee were suffering from the gravel and sharp rocks. It was brutal work to haul himself along as he was doing and he knew that his progress would become even slower with the cuts he was sustaining. He couldn't hope to make the valley before night even if his bleeding hands held out—and meanwhile thirst and hunger were beginning to take their toll.

He looked around for another corpse, thinking that he might cut up some bits of clothing to make pads for his knee and hands, but the area was now quite bare. He studied the gravel patches as he inched forward, noting that in places the marks of shod hoofs overlay moccasin tracks. Those sounds during the night had been cavalry patrols clearing the battlefield. It was a sickening thought. Help had been close but he had not dared to summon it. Evidently they had come as far as where he was now crawling but not far enough to find the bodies of the first squad men.

The morning was going rapidly now and sun's heat be-

25

gan to increase his discomfort. He got dizzy and had to rest every few feet. He tried to ignore it, telling himself that the worst was over, that he was clear of the Indians. It helped—but not much.

Two weary, painful hours passed before he reached the line of cliffs which had been the objective of L's third assault. Here he found bits of the wreckage of war, evidently in a little pocket which the searchers had missed. There were bloodstains, a broken musket of ancient model, a Cheyenne lance, a canteen and an army cartridge belt still half full of carbine ammunition. No bodies were in sight.

He tore greedily at the stopper of the canteen after shaking it to hear a light slosh from within. The water was hot but it was wet and there was a good mouthful of it. He felt better after he let it trickle down his throat. He changed the shells from the discarded belt to his own, then wrapped the empty belt around his badly lacerated crawling knee and inched ahead once more. Obviously both parties had retreated from the battlefield and probably did not propose to return, there having been no sound of movement from either side during the entire day. Maybe it wasn't going to be easy to find Crook's men.

He knew that it made no real difference to him. He had to reach water and the valley was the only place where he could find it. Water would be necessary to keep him going—and he had to keep going.

He went on, collapsing during the afternoon and falling into a troubled sleep in which his dreams became all confused. Part of the time he was riding down into New Mexico to find out what was troubling Uncle Bill. Part of the time he was riding patrol along the Santa Fe Trail with Ed Cavanagh as a fellow recruit. It all seemed so real that it was a bitter disappointment to awaken and find the pain and heat still with him. A smothering sort of darkness was beginning to fall over the silent land but the heat was still there and he ached in so many places that he found it almost impossible to move. His scraped left knee made that leg almost as useless as the wounded one. His hands were puffed and bloody, his throat parched. Maybe he wouldn't make New Mexico after all.

That was the way it had always been. Ever since he started to prove up that Homestead claim troubles had dogged him. He had kept himself broke buying land and equipment. He had used every bit of leave for the kind of hard work necessary in building cabins and sheds. Because he needed more money to keep things moving he had reenlisted—and had promptly been sent north to Wyoming where he couldn't keep an eye on the place. Today was the climax.

The bitterness brought him another small burst of energy. He couldn't quit now. Uncle Bill was still down there trying. He had to get back and see what help was needed.

Not quite knowing how he did it, he eased himself down the slope. He took a couple of bad bumps but at least he was still moving. He didn't want to think about how he would climb the second ridge.

It was well past dark when he gave up the effort. Again he slept the sleep of exhaustion, this time not rousing until dawn. His right leg seemed to be on fire and his whole body ached. He could not hope to climb the next ridge. Idly he wondered what had really been the result of the battle. He didn't know why he cared; it meant nothing to him.

He dragged himself to the shelter of some mesquite, wondering how long he could last without water. He didn't believe it would be long. Already the rocky landscape was beginning to look hazy.

He closed his eyes for a few minutes and when he opened them again he was sure delirium had got him. Not fifty feet away a half naked Indian was staring at him fixedly.

He started to pull his revolver but a flash of sanity told him that the Indian was not a Sioux. He even thought he recognized the man. Most of the Crows who had come to join Crook had been braggarts who boasted and strutted around the camp but who shirked their scouting duties, especially after that first Sioux demonstration on Tongue River. This fellow had been quite silent and he had been one of the few who had scouted diligently.

"How!" Kendrick called, using the Indian salutation

27

as best he could with lips and throat so parched that only a croak came out.

The Crow studied him for a few seconds and then took a couple of steps toward him. "Me Crow," he announced finally.

Kendrick nodded, eager to assure the man that he wasn't going to be mistaken for a hostile. "Good man," he husked, the words painful on his cracked lips. "You help. Water." He pointed to his mouth and made motions of drinking.

The Crow came to him then but it was apparent that he carried no canteen. He was a short, squatty Indian, thick bodied without being fat, a sturdy sort who wore only a breechclout, moccasins and a belt into which were thrust a knife and a keen-bladed hatchet. In his knotty brown hand he carried a well oiled Spencer repeating rifle.

He squatted down to study the crude bandage on Kendrick's thigh, paying no attention to the other injuries. Suddenly he seemed to make up his mind about something. "Bring water," he said. "Bimeby come back."

"Where is the army?" Kendrick asked, spacing the words carefully.

The Indian shook his head as he turned away. "Bimeby come back," he repeated. Then he slipped away, moving with caution as he rounded a rocky projection. It was obvious that he was alert against a possible return of the Sioux and Cheyennes.

There was nothing for Kendrick to do but wait so he made himself as comfortable as possible, hope buoying him up a little. At least he wasn't going to lie there and die of sheer hopelessness. One of Crook's scouts would certainly report him.

A good hour passed before the Indian came back, an hour which seemed at least twice as long to the feverish Kendrick. He had about made up his mind that the Indian had abandoned him when he heard the clink of a shod hoof. The stocky warrior was riding a typical Indian paint pony but he was leading two saddled cavalry mounts. There were canteens at each saddle and the Indian quickly unfastened one of them, kneeling with it to let Kendrick drink.

This time the water was plentiful enough. It was warm but it did the trick. Kendrick drank deeply once, letting another mouthful remain on his dry tongue before he swallowed it. Then the Crow took the canteen away, shaking his head warningly.

"You speak English?" Kendrick asked.

"No good." The Crow's grin was amiable.

"Maybe good enough. Where is the army?"

When the dark face showed perplexity he tried again, asking slowly, "Where white warriors? Soldiers? Where did they go?" He pointed to his own tattered uniform and to the horses, making motions to indicate the location of the troops during the battle. Then he asked again, "Where did soldiers go?"

The Indian raised his hands in front of his chest, palms turned inward, and brushed one hand against the other in an outward motion. Suddenly Kendrick remembered some of the sign language he had picked up from an old Arapaho near Fort Union. He had seen the Indians use that sign to indicate that their meat supply was exhausted. Evidently the Crow meant that the white soldiers had gone.

They worked it out from there, sign language and improvised motions supplementing the few words of English which the Crow seemed to know. It took a long time but in the end Kendrick understood that Crook had withdrawn his army from the valley of the Rosebud. Apparently the Sioux had beaten him rather badly.

While they held their odd conversation Kendrick managed to swallow some of the hard rations which the Indian produced. He found trouble in thinking clearly but for the most part he knew what he was doing.

The Indian left him after a time, leaving both cavalry horses picketed nearby and warning Kendrick by signs not to lose sight of them. The wounded man tried to keep an alert guard but dizziness proved too much for him and when he opened his eyes again the Crow was bending over him, evidently preparing to do something about the thigh wound. It was growing dark on the ridge now so he

29

judged that the Indian must have been away some three or four hours. Fortunately the horses were still safe.

The Crow went to work with some materials he had brought, spending time and effort on the inflamed thigh wound. Kendrick fainted twice while the treatment was going on but he knew that the Indian had first bathed the injuries with some sort of tea he must have been brewing while his patient slept. After that the wounds were smeared with a greasy mess whose odor was strange but not unpleasant. Finally the Indian indicated that Kendrick was now supposed to get up and start moving.

"Plenty Sioux bimeby," the squatty warrior said, pointing to the north. "Go now."

He hoisted Kendrick from the ground and lifted him to the saddle of a cavalry horse. Kendrick did not argue. He was having trouble in keeping his reeling senses from leaving him as the movement sent pain rushing through his whole body. It was the thigh that was most agonizing. He could hold on a little with the injured arm but the thigh was bad. He didn't know how bad but he feared the worst.

They moved out in the early dusk, taking a southwesterly course toward the Big Horn spur. Crook's army must have retired almost due south so it seemed likely that the scout intended to circle before approaching the army camp. Probably there were Sioux warriors hanging on the heels of the retreating troops.

After the first half mile Kendrick rode in a daze. Once he gathered his senses enough to study the stars and see that they were now moving almost due west. Still he did not ask questions. Talking was too much of an effort. He had to depend on the Crow so he might as well depend on him all the way.

They camped and slept after a time. Kendrick had no idea how much of the night had passed and he didn't care very much. He simply fell to the ground when the Indian helped him from the saddle, out cold without quite knowing what was happening.

It was a little past daybreak when the warrior aroused him again, pointing to the north and east. "Plenty Sioux," he muttered uneasily. "Go now."

They went, Kendrick still not quite sure what was happening to him. He realized that he was pretty badly fevered but he kept enough judgment to obey orders. Nothing else made sense.

Later he knew that the sun was not bothering him so much and he opened his eyes to see that they had halted in a spruce forest. For a moment he thought he was dreaming of the New Mexico mountains again but then sanity came back and he knew that they had edged into the foothills of the Big Horns. There were no spruces anywhere else in the region, so far as he knew. He tried to move and found that he was lashed to the saddle by strips of rawhide.

The Crow bobbed up beside him, grinning apologetically. "Fall off," he explained. "Bimeby fix." His motions indicated that he proposed to build a travois so that he would not have to keep his charge lashed to the saddle. Kendrick nodded, wondering when he had taken his fall. He couldn't remember it.

"How far do we go?" he asked slowly, forcing the words with a real effort of will.

He could not tell whether the Indian understood the question or not. At any rate he did not get a reply so he asked no more questions. Words were too hard to get out.

There was an interval in which he watched the swift fashioning of the travois but then the blackness came again and he knew no more until he felt himself being lashed fast to it. This time he could not find the strength to ask a question so he let the dizziness engulf him. Twice after that he roused briefly to the agonies of the jolting ride but there was a merciful vagueness in his mind. He wasn't sure where he was or what was happening to him.

4

KENDRICK roused from the longest and most terrifying nightmare of his life to a sensation of smell. He enjoyed the smell for a few minutes before he opened his eyes. Several times he had known pleasant sensations only to open his eyes for a little while and find only pain and trouble. Now he was reluctant to drive away anything that seemed good.

Still he forced himself to do it and this time the results were not bad. He looked up at twinkling stars in a blue-black sky and when he turned his head he could see a dozen small fires close at hand, most of them blazing merrily under cooking pots or bits of roasting meat. That was where the wonderful smell was coming from.

He was in an Indian camp, he knew, but apparently it was a camp well removed from any fighting zone. There were women bustling about the cooking chores, their manner cheerful and almost careless as though they had no fear than an enemy might sight the fires and attack. Only a couple of warriors appeared in the camp and they were showing no signs of worry either. Kendrick decided that all was well. He was hungry—which was even better.

None of the Indians was close to him so he took time to look around, seeing immediately that he had been getting good care. A lean-to of heavy boughs sheltered him although he could see plenty of sky. He was lying on a blanket under which several hides had been placed as a sort of mattress. He moved his hands and found that he was weak but in control of himself. And the movement did not bring any pain. He had improved miraculously.

Then he raised a trembling hand to his mouth and part of the miracle was explained. His beard was noticeably longer than it had been when he last felt it. Apparently he had been out of his head for quite a long time.

One of the women must have seen the movement for

he heard a voice call out something in a tongue he could not understand and a warrior came over toward him at once. He was a young man, very tall and with a skin so light that Kendrick put him down as a half-breed. When he spoke the guess sounded all the more accurate.

"Feeling better, trooper?" he asked, his voice carrying a hint of the South. "You slept a long time."

"How long?" Kendrick asked.

"Five-six days, I understand. I came in three days ago and they told me you'd been here a couple of days before that. Cloud said you'd been out of your head a day or so before he hauled you this far." The Indian spoke easily as though thoroughly accustomed to the language.

"Is Cloud the man who brought me from the battlefield?"

"That's right. Cloud-on-the-Mountain. I'm Tall Elk. They tagged me as Henry Martin at the reservation school. Cloud lit out as soon as he turned you over to the squaws; wasn't taking any chances on having you get well and claim the horses from him, I reckon." He laughed.

"Where am I?" Kendrick asked.

"Crow village along the northwest angle of the Big Horns. Take it easy now and I'll get one of the women to bring you some stew. You'll need a lot if it after so many days with nothing but a sip of broth now and then."

He went away and presently a wrinkled old crone came over with some hot stew in a battered iron pot. She looked dirty and so did the pot but Kendrick was in no mood to be particular. The stew savored of herbs he did not recognize and its taste was as good as its odor. He ate as much of it as the old woman would let him have and then he drowsed off again, reassured that his wounds must be healing rapidly; there was little pain, even when he moved the injured right leg. The squatty Indian's medicine must have been remarkably effective.

The squaw fed him again later in the evening and he slept a long natural sleep, awakening to find the dawn well broken and the camp lazily astir. Evidently the fighting was of little concern to this village.

Tall Elk came to talk with him when the same old

woman brought him a breakfast of some sort of porridge and more stew. This time Kendrick was able to get a little more information from the good natured halfbreed. He learned that most of the warriors belonging to this village were still with General Crook although a few had gone to take employment with either Custer or Gibbon.

"Had any report on that fight where I got busted up?" Kendrick asked. "My impression was that our side got the worst of a fight that was still mostly a standoff."

The halfbreed nodded soberly. "All I know is what Cloud-on-the-Mountain told me when he brought you into camp. He claims your general missed his chance and that Crazy Horse missed a better one. Neither side was real anxious to follow up the fight."

"Which is how it happened that I got picked up, I suppose."

"That's right. Cloud was one of the few who took a chance on scouting the field next day."

Kendrick knew that Cloud had probably been in search of loot but he didn't say so. The Indian had undoubtedly saved his life so he was in no mood to make comments about the cavalry horses or the weapons which had come into the possession of the small warrior. He asked how Cloud had figured that both sides missed their chances, thinking he might pick up a bit of information that he could take back with him.

The tall man squatted lithely, apparently quite willing to talk. "Your army was supposed to attack the Sioux—but not alone. Is that right?"

"That's what we heard in the ranks."

"No secret. You were to pinch the Sioux between your force and the armies of Terry and Gibbon. So your big aim was to keep pushing until you had them trapped. Instead your General Crook sat down and waited for Crazy Horse to do the pushing. Then you had to fight a defensive battle. When it was over your men pulled back and let the Sioux ride off into the north to strengthen the forces opposing Custer and Terry and Gibbon. Cloud and me figure that makes Crook's campaign a failure."

"Then the general has really retreated?"

34

"So I hear. At least he's stopped pushing. I haven't had any real report for the past couple of days."

Kendrick shook his head. "I keep forgetting how much time has passed. Got any idea what the date is?"

"Twenty-fourth, I believe. We don't pay much attention to calendars around here." His grin was drily humorous.

"So what about Crazy Horse? What was his mistake?"

"He laid a trap and then let his warriors scare you out of it."

"How's that again?"

"I'm just repeating what Cloud told me. The Sioux had an ambush for any of your men who would attack their village. Somewhere during the battle a part of your army went to hit the village but before they could get into the trap another lot of Indians attacked your lines at the valley and the men heading into the trap were called back to stop the attack behind them. That spoiled the whole show from the Sioux standpoint."

Kendrick thought about it, remembering how he had listened to those bugle calls in the afternoon. Mills's battalion had been sent somewhere but had been called back. It fitted with what Tall Elk was saying. "Where is General Crook now?" he asked finally.

"Last report had him camped along the northeast base of the Big Horns. That was a couple of days ago but the report was that he was moving back still farther, taking his supplies and wounded. He may be on his way back to the Powder by this time."

"I've got to get back to the army."

"You've lost a lot of blood and the fever didn't do you a bit of good. You can't travel for a long time yet—and you're lucky. This fight might get worse before it gets better. That's why our people have moved so far to the west."

On the following day Kendrick did not see Tall Elk in the camp but the women continued to take good care of him and he found that he could sit up for a few minutes at a time without too much distress. It was obvious that

35

he wouldn't be able to walk for some days to come but at least he was recovering.

He began to fret over his helplessness. The days were passing and the date of his discharge was coming along. Instead of being ready for his move back into civilian life he was tucked away in a remote Indian camp, unable to contact the army and probably reported as killed in action.

The latter thought bothered him particularly. Probably some notification would reach Uncle Bill in due time and the old man would be needlessly troubled. Moreover there could be lots of complications with army red tape.

Another day passed with no sign of activity around the camp but that evening a dozen warriors came in on jaded ponies, their excited talk hinting that something big had developed. Kendrick couldn't make head or tail of it but shortly after dusk another weary band came in, this lot being accompanied by Tall Elk.

The mysterious halfbreed came over to Kendrick at once. "Bad news," he said grimly. "Long-hair Custer was wiped out."

"No!"

"It's true. Four warriors from this village were with him and three of them came back. Custer split his regiment and hit the big camp of Sitting Bull with about half of his men. Our boys ducked out when it got rough and they claim none of Custer's men lived through it. Now it seems as though the Sioux are ready for General Gibbon and the rest of Terry's force."

Kendrick didn't know what to say. Crook thrown back and Custer wiped out! Two disasters in a week. It seemed almost impossible but he had seen the fury of the Sioux-Cheyenne attacks above the Rosebud valley. It must have happened that way. Certainly the Crows accepted the word without doubt. Two white armies had been defeated and their Crow allies were worried.

Far into the night the council fires burned, Tall Elk interpreting for Kendrick. The scouts who had been with Crook reported him in full retreat southward. Terry's column was in danger after the loss of Custer's command. Gibbon's location was not known to the Crows. If the Sioux had been able to defeat and disorganize three white armies it seemed likely that they would use their moment of triumph to expand their campaign and aim a mortal blow at their old enemies the Crows and Shoshones. The northern Big Horns would be no place for the people of either tribe.

An hour before dawn the Indians were busy at the task of breaking camp, their movements speeded by the report of a new scout that the Sioux were already gone from the valley of the Little Big Horn. Gibbon's men had come down from the north but the hostiles had not waited to meet him, scattering on purposes of their own instead of forcing a third big battle. It was presumed that the triumphant Indians would now raid in all directions.

Kendrick was given a horse and helped to mount but otherwise left to get along as best he could. He could sense a division of feeling toward him among the Indians, some of them scorning him openly as a representative of a defeated and humbled tribe while others offered small bits of assistance as though looking forward to a time when other white soldiers would come to retrieve the disasters.

Kendrick almost enjoyed the first couple of miles of the march but then the jolting brought back the pain and dizziness so that he had to hang on blindly to the pony's mane. For what seemed like weeks he rode in that condition, sometimes thinking that he was charging the Sioux on the heights above the Rosebud and sometimes that he was riding a patrol along the Santa Fe Trail.

Once his mind cleared enough for him to talk with Tall Elk at a night camp, learning that the Indians had put two full days behind them. They were moving southwest away from the dangerous Big Horn country, proposing to hunt along the Wind River Range while their regular haunts were subject to raid.

Two days after that conversation the band set up their tepees in a sheltered valley and Kendrick was left to recuperate as best he could, fed by the same wrinkled squaw but otherwise ignored. It bothered him a little that he had not seen Cloud again. Undoubtedly he owed his life to the squatty warrior and he had not even thanked him.

It took a week for him to get back to the state of recovery he had enjoyed before this retreat and even then he found it impossible to take more than a few steps without breaking out into a sweat of exhaustion. He still had a free foot around the camp but mostly the Crows paid little attention to him. He talked with Elk a couple of times, learning that Crook's force was being reorganized with infantry units. The Indians didn't think much of the idea. If Long-Hair Custer and the famous Seventh Cavalry could be wiped out by the Sioux it didn't make much sense to attack with foot soldiers. At any rate the Crows did not propose to ally themselves with such forces.

Kendrick did not bother himself with details. The only important point was that his regiment was still somewhere east of the Big Horns. He had to reach it soon or there would be a fine mess of red tape to untangle. Already July was passing rapidly.

As soon as he felt that he could ride he tried to make arrangements to head east but Tall Elk did not come to the mountain camp and Kendrick wasn't able to make himself understood to any of the other Crows. They were friendly enough when he tried casual sign language conversations but when he touched on the subject of horses or firearms they went dumb. He took the hint and decided to wait for Elk.

He figured that July was about gone when he saw signs of restlessness in the camp. The Crows were getting ready to move. Picking an old chief who had been a little more cordial than some of the others Kendrick announced his intention of leaving. The old man agreed promptly, suddenly finding English words with which to express himself reasonably well. It was a good time to go, he told Kendrick. The Sioux threat was over. The Crows could go back to their usual hunting grounds.

There was no explanation of this change of situation but Kendrick did not press for one. He was more interested in the matter of getting a horse and a gun. On that point the chief was apologetic. No ponies could be spared. The white warrior's gun would be returned to him but there would be no horse for him to ride.

On the following day his Colt's revolver was brought to him, all six of its chambers loaded but with no extra cartridges being produced. He tried to sound the Indians out on the subject of extra shells. It was clear that he wouldn't get his carbine back but he hoped that spare ammunition might be forthcoming.

It proved to be a hopeless task. There were no extra shells in the camp, or so the Indians pretended. Two mornings later the Crows broke camp and pushed off to the north, leaving Kendrick to head in the opposite direction on foot. He had a pair of decent buckskin trousers, his own patched shirt, his campaign hat, a pair of broken cavalry boots, a small skin of pemmican and a loaded six-shooter. Somewhere south of him was the Overland Trail.

5

NEARLY three weeks later he made camp in a draw where deep wagon ruts marked a main trail. This would be the Overland, he felt sure, the stream just beyond it being the Sweetwater. He had never been in the region but that was the way he remembered the maps. At the moment he didn't care very much.

The hike south had been a continuing nightmare, his weakness not permitting him to travel fast even though he realized that speed meant a lot. With only six cartridges he had to complete the journey while he still had the means of getting food. On that score he had been fortunate, his kills coming at times when he could lie over to recuperate while he ate at leisure. Still he was bone-tired when he hit the Sweetwater. His boots were now no more than frames on which to tie strips of deerskin. His revolver still contained one cartridge but he had been without food for nearly two days.

It was cold that night, the chill in the air reminding him that the summer was moving along rapidly. Still he slept well, having indulged in the luxury of a good bath in the river. After the weeks in the Crow camp and on the trail it was something he needed almost as badly as he needed food and rest.

At dawn he struck it rich. A buck mule deer came down to the stream to drink, pausing within thirty feet of the willow clump where Kendrick had been sleeping. The Colt's last slug knocked him over and Kendrick jumped in with his knife to make sure of his prize.

An hour later a train of Mormon freight wagons headed for Utah came in sight and he hailed them, telling his story and getting some news in return. The big Indian campaign was still continuing although the Sioux had broken up into small bands, probably because their leaders couldn't hold them together. Some Sioux were supposed to be heading for Canada and Crook's army was now on the trail of the villages remaining in the country. There had been a fight on Warbonnet Creek which had kept the main force of Cheyennes from joining the Sioux and the big threat seemed to be over.

More important than information was the quick trade Kendrick made with the Mormons. In return for the fresh meat he was able to provide he received a warm jacket, a new pair of boots and an invitation to ride along until they could meet wagons heading east. It seemed like a better risk than continued walking so Kendrick went along.

He rode with them for the balance of the day and part of the next, regaining his strength quickly with the rest and better food. In the middle of the second afternoon they met a train of army wagons moving east from Fort Bridger to Fort Laramie so Kendrick left the Mormons and reported himself to the bored lieutenant in charge of the wagon train. The officer clearly believed Kendrick to be a deserter who had grown tired of living with the Indians but he agreed to take him along.

"I'll turn you over to the commander at Fort Fetterman," he said shortly. "He can figure out what ought to be done about you. It's none of my business."

It was almost the last thing he said to Kendrick. The train rolled slowly eastward along the Sweetwater and

North Platte, reaching Fort Fetterman on the last day of August, a good six weeks past the day when Kendrick's retirement should have become effective. By that time delay had ceased to mean anything. Getting back was all that counted.

At Fetterman there was no one who had ever heard of Kendrick. General Crook's records and equipment had been moved from this former base and no one knew what had happened to them. The commandant obviously suspected Kendrick of being a deserter, even when he saw the barely healed bullet wounds. Like the commissary lieutenant he did not want to be bothered with the problem so he ordered Kendrick sent on to Fort Laramie with the empty wagons.

At Laramie matters were no happier. Crook's regiment was now supposed to be somewhere in the Black Hills but nobody seemed to care very much. It was believed that the regimental records had been sent to Fort D. A. Russell so Kendrick was sent to that post under custody of a mail escort. By that time he knew he was being considered as a prisoner. It was now October, much too late to make any move southward into New Mexico. He managed to write a letter to Uncle Bill, reporting himself alive in case a false report of his death had been sent out, but then he could do nothing but go along to Fort Russell and hope that somebody in the army would be willing to look into his case. The Third Cavalry certainly must have its records on file somewhere.

At Fort Russell the luck turned. He was turned over to a Captain Lowry who wore the insignia of the Ninth Infantry on his trim blue uniform. The man looked thin and rather sour but his manner was decent enough as he returned Kendrick's salute.

"You claim to be an enlisted man of the Third Cavalry, cut off from your detachment at the battle of the Rosebud, I understand. Do you have any way of proving yourself?"

"May I ask a question, sir?"

"Of course."

"Were you with the Ninth at the Rosebud?"

A quizzical smile showed on the officer's face. "I was.

41

That's how it happens that I'm here now. I stopped a bullet."

"Then you were with the—jackass cavalry along the base of the first ridge when the fight started?"

"We'll overlook the term. Go on." He was grinning a little more broadly now and Kendrick felt better.

"I was with Troop L of the Third. We passed through your picket line when we made the first charge. Your men closed up behind us and helped with our casualties."

"So far you're correct. I even remember the names of a couple of your men that we brought back. Can you tell me who they were?"

"My squad lost one, sir. A young fellow named Michaels."

"That's correct. We brought Michaels in but I'm afraid he's dead."

Kendrick nodded. "I'm the only survivor, I believe. The others were killed in the pocket where I was trapped."

An orderly came in at that point, saluting as he announced, "We went over the lists, sir. There is a man from the Third Cavalry still in the hospital here. He's able to move around well enough."

"Bring him along," the captain ordered.

He nodded a little more easily toward Kendrick as he explained, "We're trying to square this thing up as best we can. Maybe the man my orderly mentions won't know you, particularly since your immediate unit seems to have been wiped out but we'll see what happens. Just sit down there and wait until he arrives."

Ten minutes later a little man in fatigues was brought in, a man who limped on his left foot but who otherwise seemed quite fit and in good spirits. He exchanged amazed glances with Kendrick but quickly wiped away the smile and saluted briskly. "You sent for me, sir?" he asked the captain.

"I did. Do you know this man?"

"Yes, sir."

"His name, rank and unit?"

"Corporal Tom Kendrick, Third United States Cavalry, sir. If I may add a word, sir, Corporal Kendrick was reported killed at the Rosebud. I made the original report."

When the officer nodded his agreement Trooper Smith dropped his formality and asked, "Your permission, sir?" Then without waiting for a reply he turned to grab Kendrick's hand. "Where in hell have you been?" he demanded. "And how did you get away? I saw you go down."

"Sit down, both of you," the infantry captain ordered. "I think it's time three lucky survivors of a tough fight hashed over a few details." His sour look had disappeared entirely and Kendrick knew the worst was over. Now there would be only the matter of untangling the red tape. With an officer to help out that shouldn't be too much of a problem.

They took plenty of time, many matters having to be explained on all sides, but eventually Kendrick got his story told. In return he learned that Smith had been the only member of the first squad to fight his way out of the trap, going down with a bullet in his leg just as help arrived. Practically all of Troop L had been cut off for a few minutes but after some sharp fighting they had regained the line which was then formed on the third ridge. Smith knew nothing of the subsequent fighting but Captain Lowry was able to supply the facts that corroborated the accounts Tall Elk had brought to Kendrick. The Rosebud had been a disaster but not as great a disaster as it might have been had the Cheyenne warriors carried out the strategy of Crazy Horse.

With identification cleared up Kendrick could do nothing but wait. Captain Lowry took charge of the whole matter, showing a great deal of energy and proving to be a real friend. However he could do no more than get the wheels to turning. Records would have to be altered at several military posts, probably all the way to Washington. It would take time to get a proper discharge for a man who had been listed as killed. Kendrick hoped that the added delay would not make matters worse for Uncle Bill but that was all he could do. Hope.

Winter settled down on Fort Russell and Kendrick carried out the light duties which had been assigned to him, gradually recovering his strength. In early November Crook's army was reported at Fort Robinson and some facts of interest filtered through in the mails. Sergeant Cavanagh had handled the reporting of casualties from the Rosebud and had also disposed of the dead men's personal effects. Cavanagh had not reenlisted and his whereabouts were unknown.

"Uncle Bill's been notified," Kendrick told Smith. "Ed knew about Uncle Bill so he would have sent everything down there. I hope my letter got to him in time to relieve the strain a little."

In December Smith got his discharge on disability. He promptly moved from the fort into the winter-bound town of Cheyenne and Kendrick did not see him for nearly two months. Fort gossip said that the little man was doing well by himself as a faro dealer in one of the town's numerous gambling halls and Kendrick recalled the old rumor that Smith had once been a Mississippi River gambler. Probably it was true. Plenty of men ducked away from law troubles by enlisting in the army under assumed names.

Shortly after the first of the year Captain Lowry's efforts began to bring results. The name of Corporal Thomas Kendrick was restored to the rolls and warrants for back pay were ordered drawn. Less than a week later other orders arrived providing for his honorable discharge and for full pay beyond the proper discharge date. Suddenly Kendrick found himself out of the army with a substantial sum of money in his pocket. At last he was ready to head south. Or he would have been if there had been any possibility of making the journey. With snow blanketing the country he could do nothing but continue the waiting game.

It worried him a little that he had heard nothing from Uncle Bill but he knew that mail from New Mexico was a haphazard affair. Probably the word of his supposed death had not reached Uncle Bill until late autumn. His own letter might not have been delivered until winter. Anyway Uncle Bill would not have known where to send any reply.

He moved into Cheyenne in early February, quickly arranging to share a room with Smith. The little man was evidently prosperous and had developed something

44

of a reputation in town. Everyone called him Mac and he announced with some pride that it was short for Mac-Beth. Apparently he was back at his old habit of quoting Shakespeare.

For Kendrick the next month was something of an education. He picked up a couple of odd jobs to keep himself going without touching his capital, spending the evenings with Smith's books while the little man worked at his job in the gambling house. Neither of them talked about the future but when Kendrick began to collect equipment for his move south Smith declared his intention of going along.

"I figure I owe you something, Tom," the little man said quietly. "In a way I put you in a bad spot, deserting you the way I did and reporting you killed. Maybe I can help you along now. I've got a bit of capital and I'm thinking it'll come in handy if that country's opening up the way you say it is."

"You don't owe me a thing," Kendrick told him. "It was lucky for me you happened to be on hand to identify me when you did. But I'll be glad to have you along if you're not anxious to stick with your job here."

Smith chuckled. "I'll be safer in New Mexico. Sooner or later somebody will come along who'll remember a small sized character who spouts a bit from the bard now and then. It could be embarrassing if word got back to certain lawmen along the big river. I killed a man back there, you know."

Kendrick shook his head. "I didn't know."

"It's nothing on my conscience. The dirty crook had it coming to him and it was either him or me—but that wasn't the way the law looked at it. Anyway, I'll be just as well off to keep shady."

Kendrick chuckled. "You're in, Mac. A broken-down cavalryman and an old Mississippi three-card-monte man —just what New Mexico needs!"

That settled it. They left Cheyenne when the first trains began to move on the new rail line down into Colorado. In Denver they transferred to the Santa Fe and at Pueblo they bought horses and moved on south through the mud of spring. For a time Kendrick felt a sense of disquiet, the country being so unfamiliar to him. When he had seen it last there had been only the wagon trails but now the Santa Fe was grading southward, inching toward Raton Pass where work crews were already beginning to hack out a climb that would be possible for locomotives. After nearly eight years of surveys and talk the line was going through.

"It's what we hoped for in the beginning," he told Smith as they passed the labor gangs. "When they run rail to Santa Fe we'll be close enough to the line so that our place will amount to something. We'll be able to get produce out to market."

"Not much farm country around here," Smith commented. "It's mostly bare gravel with a bit of poor grazing land."

"That's what makes our valley so valuable. We're up away from the dry prairie but not far enough up to be in the real mountains. We've got good water, good grass, and good timber. Not many places in the southwest can match that combination." He grinned a little as he added, "I suppose I'm getting to sound real enthused. After all, I've been a long while waiting for this."

They crossed Raton Pass and worked through more of the flat country, coming at last to a region where mountains loomed dark in the west. A couple of fresh running streams hinted that the mountains were providing water for this land to the east but Kendrick was not impressed. "Dry in summer," he said briefly. "Up Packsaddle Creek we've got good water all the time. You'll see."

"How come nobody else has moved in on you?"

"Probably they have by this time. I heard from Uncle Bill three years ago about a big English-owned cow outfit that had started to move into the territory north of our place. Since then they've had some gold talk off to the west. Between the two that ought to mean something stirring."

That afternoon they rode into high country again, Kendrick picking a way where no trail existed. He was forcing the pace now and Smith called him on it.

Kendrick eased back a little, letting the horses walk. "Not far ahead," he explained, "this rocky plateau breaks

46

down into Packsaddle Valley. I was hoping I might get a look at the place before dark but there's no point in straining too hard."

Just at dusk they halted to study a well marked trail of a cattle drive. Someone had moved a sizable bunch of steers through here, moving from northwest to southeast. Kendrick tracked it backward a short distance but then reined aside to make camp in a shallow draw. "Funny kind of trail," he muttered to the smaller man. "It seems to come out of the country where this big outfit was supposed to be setting up shop but I don't see why they would move stock this way. It's tough going."

"Eastern market?" Smith suggested.

"Maybe. But it would be easier to drive down the creek. Uncle Bill said he'd made a deal to let them go through. I'll have to ask him about this."

They camped a little to the west of the cattle trace, neither of them talking much as they made supper and turned in for the night. Smith was too weary for idle chatter and Kendrick too worried. He didn't like the look of that cattle trail. Uncle Bill had mentioned the arrival of the big English syndicate which had begun to run a lot of stock in the region. Maybe there was a connection between the arrival of a cattle outfit and the hint of trouble. Uncle Bill hadn't said so but it was a likely tie-up. Cattlemen and homesteaders had locked horns before.

THEY broke camp at dawn, taking time only for coffee. "We'll eat with Uncle Bill," Kendrick said with a broad smile of anticipation. He had gotten rid of his beard and mustache while at Fort Russell, looking several years younger than he had appeared on the Rosebud.

"You're kinda perked up for this, I gather," Smith said dryly.

"After five years? I should say so! We'll bust in on Uncle Bill and have ourself some real grub."

Twenty minutes later they could see the rim of rocks ahead of them with only sky showing beyond. Pine-clad ridges lay beyond the opening but Kendrick was not looking that far. His only interest at the moment was in what lay just below the rim.

"Easy does it," he warned. "There's a sharp drop ahead. We'll angle down a little piece over there to the right but I'd like to take a look first."

They pulled up together and Kendrick pointed into the green valley which opened up ahead of them to the south and southwest. "This is it," he said proudly. "The buildings just below us are Uncle Bill's. My homestead claim is on the other side of the creek at the foot of the next ridge. You can see my cabin over there at the edge of the pines."

"How much land?" Smith asked.

"The usual hundred and sixty acres. In my case, though, I own a big strip just west of both quarter sections and on up to the north. It's one of those Spanish strips I bought from a down-and-out hidalgo who was too proud to look around for ways of working it. I don't know how much good it will be to me but it was cheap so I bought it from him."

"What's a Spanish strip?" Smith asked.

"One of the narrow strips of land resulting from divisions of the original Spanish grants. The old Spaniards were big land owners—in land that never belonged to them, of course—and their usual unit was about a hundred square miles. Their heirs gradually divided the tracts, always running lines north and south through the whole grant. After a couple of centuries some of the tracts became broken up into crazy patterns, the individual holdings all being ten miles from north to south but pretty narrow from east to west. The piece I bought runs ten miles north from a spot just below the southwest corner of my homestead quarter-section but less than a mile west from it. Its width is one-twelfth of ten miles." He pointed across the valley. "It's the first ridge over there and some broken country to the north of it."

Smith nodded his understanding and Kendrick went on quickly, his flow of talk partly an indication of the excitement he felt. "Not a bit of ground turned over yet. Uncle Bill ought to have thirty acres plowed by this time. Maybe something's wrong."

"Let's get moving," the little man suggested. "You won't learn anything very important by sitting up here and worrying."

Kendrick swung his mount aside, leading the way to a steep path which angled down the sharp slope into the valley. Scrub cedars screened a large part of the descent and for several minutes they had no further look at the valley. Then the path became still more rocky and the screening trees thinned out. Kendrick emitted a sudden grunt of astonishment and pulled up short. Down below him four riders were spurring hard toward the log house, apparently having just broken out of the timber along the upper creek.

"Hello!" he exclaimed. "Now what are they up to?"

Mac snapped, "They look ugly to me—and there's a woman coming out of the house with a gun. You didn't tell me your uncle was married."

Kendrick took a longer look and then put spurs to his horse, turning his head to yell, "He's not. Let's go!"

He took the rest of the descent at a dangerous clip. There was a good stand of pine at the base of the cliff so he lost sight of the riders for several minutes while he was working his way out from the slope to the flat country of the valley proper. When he saw them again he knew that he had struck something pretty nasty. The four men were driving down on a little bunch of cattle, firing as they rode. The woman had halted at a little distance, kneeling to fire grimly at the raiders with her rifle. She was defending Uncle Bill Hockett's little beef herd.

Kendrick pulled his six-gun as he spurred the black toward the raiders, shoving in a sixth cartridge to give him as much fire power as possible. He saw the raiders circle after shooting down three steers, apparently aiming for a second bunch of steers a little farther away from the woman and her rifle. Kendrick changed direction and rode to intercept. He knew that Mac Smith had dropped

49

far behind but for the moment his anger was stronger than any thoughts of caution.

He was almost within range when they spotted him, two of the raiders whirling their mounts to meet his attack. One of them, a lean little man in faded levis, opened fire at once but the bearded fellow behind him crouched low in the saddle as though to drive in for a sure kill. Kendrick blasted a pair of shots at the little man and saw him swerve away. Then he drew fire on the more distant but seemingly more dangerous enemy. The bearded man was raising his gun now, trying to line its sight over the ears of his running horse. Kendrick fired, steadied and fired again, aware that two slugs had whined dangerously close to his head.

The bearded rider was closing fast now so Kendrick tried to beat him to the good shot, pulling up suddenly and picking the brief moment of steadiness to trigger a really aimed shot. The other man fired at the same moment and Kendrick knew that both bullets had struck home. He heard the man's curse of dismay and he felt the twinge of pain along his own lower ribs. Then the enemy was in full retreat, holding to his saddle horn with the same hand that still held a gun.

Kendrick tried to reload but for a moment or two his fingers were all thumbs. Then he knew that the emergency was over. Smith was coming up behind him with his gun blazing and the four raiders were making a hard run for the cover of the upper valley timber.

He holstered his gun and ran his hand around to the left side of his body, feeling the wet spot where blood was beginning to run down across his belt. Not much of a wound, he thought. He had survived worse ones.

"Hurt bad?" Smith demanded, pulling up beside him.

"Just a crease. No trouble."

"What the devil was going on here? Got any idea?"

"Not the least. But Uncle Bill wasn't just talking through his hat when he hinted that trouble was stirring. I reckon we'd better go ask a couple of questions. The lady with the rifle might know some answers."

"Who is she?"

50

"That's one of the things we'll ask. Uncle Bill's a bachelor."

They turned their horses and started back toward the spot where the woman stood waiting, anger showing in her very stance. Kendrick saw that she was not very old, probably in her middle twenties. The shapeless house dress had marked her only as a woman when he had seen her at a distance but now he saw that she had a nicely rounded but youthful figure—and a pretty face. Heavy brogans suggested that she did other chores in addition to housework but she was certainly not the typical frontier drudge. Her soft brown hair was neatly arranged on a well shaped head and her smooth complexion held a hint of early spring tan. Anger glowed in her dark eyes.

"Hope we didn't chase any friends away, ma'am," he greeted, probing gently for some sort of explanation.

"Thanks for helping," she said, trying to control her anger. "Did you manage to hit any of the dirty scoundrels?"

"I tagged one for sure," Kendrick replied. "A big hombre with a lot of whiskers. Maybe I even nicked the little one. What's going on around here?"

"They're trying to drive me away," she said bitterly. "They think they can scare me off by killing my stock. It's too bad I didn't see them sooner. I didn't manage to get within good rifle range."

She shook the rifle significantly and Kendrick stared. The weapon she held was one he had given to Uncle Bill six years earlier. There could be no mistaking it. Very few of those fifty-caliber Navy Springfields ever found their way to the border, especially when the forty-five bore made them practically obsolete. This particular gun had come into Kendrick's hands after an Apache raid on a wagon train and he had kept it for Uncle Bill because it was in excellent condition. He could see the anchor symbol on it and an odd knurl in the stock. It was Uncle Bill's rifle, sure enough.

"Killing your stock?" he repeated slowly, stressing the possessive. "I thought this place belonged to a man named Hockett."

51

"It did." Her voice was still grim. "Mr. Hockett was killed last summer. By this same set of rascals, I'm sure."

He heard Smith's little grunt of surprise but before he could find words to express himself the woman exclaimed, "You're wounded! I didn't know."

"Scratch," he told her. "I'll be all right."

Her voice changed swiftly. "You ride straight to the house," she directed. "I'll attend to that injury at once." Then looking up at Smith she went on, "You there. Swing over there and make sure that any of those wounded brutes are put out of their misery. Then come back to the house; I may need your help."

Kendrick saw that Mac was staring in mixed amazement and perplexity. Giving the little man a warning frown he said, "Take care of it, will you, Mac? And keep an eye out in case the devils come back."

The girl was already trotting toward the log house, her rifle trailing at her side. Kendrick followed, dismounting at the back door and looping his reins over the hitch rack he had built for Uncle Bill. The wound in his side did not bother him half as much as the news he had just heard. So Uncle Bill was dead! What had happened here in this peaceful valley? Who was the grim young woman who seemed to have taken charge of the place?

"Inside," the girl directed as he swung from the saddle. "You're feeling all right to walk, aren't you?"

"I told you it's no more than a scratch. I've had plenty worse ones."

"In the army?"

"Yes. Why did you ask?"

"I noticed your trousers. Blue with a trace where a stripe has been removed. Cavalry?"

"You've got good eyes."

She shrugged as she led the way into the house. "I knew what to look for. My husband wore trousers just like them."

"*Wore* them," he repeated. "Does that mean he . . . ?"

"My husband was shot down six months ago just as it happened to his uncle last summer. All part of this same dirty . . . "

It was his turn to interrupt. "Bill Hockett was your

husband's uncle? That . . . " This time he let the sentence trail off. Maybe this wasn't the time to start asking too many questions.

She turned to face him just inside the kitchen door, some of the pain and anger leaving her features as she showed a new interest. "Maybe you knew my husband. Since you were also in the cavalry and knew Mr. Hockett, that is. He was Corporal Tom Kendrick of the Third Cavalry."

Kendrick began to wonder whether his wound might not be worse than he had supposed. Maybe he was getting delirious again. He swallowed hard and hurried past her, cautiously rounding the big kitchen range to make for the inside pump which he had helped Uncle Bill to install. Finding it where he expected it to be helpful a little but he still wasn't sure of himself even after he splashed cold water on his face.

"Let's get that shirt off," the girl proposed anxiously. "I'm afraid you're hurt worse than you let on."

Kendrick stripped off his shirt and undershirt, revealing a small furrow about three inches above his belt line, a mere dig in the lean meat across his rib. It had bled a little but it wasn't a wound to put a man out of action— or out of his head. Apparently he had been hearing correctly, all the more reason to keep quiet and find out what this mysterious business meant.

"Not really bad," the girl declared after inspecting the injury and cleaning it out. "Shock and excitement worse than the wound, I suppose. You'd better take it easy until it wears off."

He let her order him around as she pleased, waiting for her to take up the subject which interested him so much but which he didn't want to press on his own account. He even agreed to lie down for a while when she insisted on it.

She dressed the wound, showed him to a bunk which he knew had been altered a great deal since Uncle Bill had used it. Then she swung away quickly. "Stay right there and rest," she ordered. "Your friend can take care of things outside. I'll go tell him what needs to be done."

Capable, he decided. In spite of her troubles, past and

53

present, she knew what she was doing every minute. He wished he could say the same for himself.

He tried to make some sense out of the pattern of confusion that had presented itself. Uncle Bill had been killed during the past summer, probably during the period when Kendrick had been with the Crows. Someone had turned up to claim the estate of the dead man, someone who had passed himself off as Tom Kendrick. Now the woman who claimed to be the widow of this false Tom Kendrick was apparently the presumed owner of the homestead. That took a lot of explaining. Somebody had made a lot of fast, bold moves—and had made them in the face of a deadly opponent who hadn't hesitated to commit two murders and to continue with such a daylight raid as the recent one. Kendrick was glad he had not revealed his own identity. It might be plenty smart to keep that as an ace in the hole. Probably he would need it— and more.

7

AFTER a little while he heard the girl come back into the kitchen. She did not speak to him and once there was a smothered sniffle as she busied herself out there. Kendrick decided that she was entitled to that much after all that had been happening to her, even though the evidence indicated that she was a party to some kind of fraud.

For the moment that was the most confusing part of the whole mess, he thought. He wanted to know more about the death of Uncle Bill. He wanted to know what had started a feud that would result in two murders and a raid against a nester's cattle. But he couldn't ask too many questions until he knew more about the other part of the puzzle. How had this girl become the apparent owner of Uncle Bill's homestead?

He remained on the bunk until she came in with a mug of hot coffee. If she had actually been crying she didn't show it, her smile quite cheerful as she asked, "Are you ready for something like this, soldier?"

He sat up gingerly, ignoring her protest and moving to a straight-backed chair where he could rest the coffee cup on his knee. "I imagine Mac could use some of this," he told her. "Neither of us had much breakfast."

"Mac?" she questioned, a little sharply. "He told me his name was Smith."

Kendrick chuckled. "Smith's the name he used in the army, but I don't suppose it's his real one. The boys at Cheyenne called him Mac. That's short for MacBeth. Smith's a great hand for spouting bright remarks by a fellow named Shakespeare."

"Oh, no!" she exclaimed, her wail obviously false. "It's going to be awful when he meets my father. One Shakespeare addict around here is enough."

"Where is your father?"

"In Packsaddle. He runs an assay office there."

"Maybe we can keep the pair of them separated." He was smiling with her now, the strain of the past hour suddenly gone.

"I've already spoiled that possibility. I just sent your friend MacBeth to meet Falstaff—if you get what I mean."

"You sent Mac after your father?"

"Partly. I sent him to Packsaddle mostly to summon a butchering crew. We can salvage something by having those dead animals skinned out and turned into beef without delay. Mr. Trappe supplies beef to several mining camps and freight outfits around here so he'll be glad to buy the beef, I'm sure."

"Where is Packsaddle?" Kendrick asked, keeping away from the subject of Amos Trappe.

"About five miles down the creek. I suppose the place didn't even exist when you were around here last?"

"That's right. I did hear that Trappe had moved up into the hills away from his old stand along the Santa Fe Trail but I didn't know there was any particular name for the new spot."

"Then you know Mr. Trappe?"

He shrugged. "I knew who he was—same as I did several other traders. We weren't familiar."

Some of the suspicion came back into her voice. "Your friend claimed he didn't know Trappe."

"He didn't. Smith wasn't with the regiment when we were down this way. He joined us after we went up into Dakotah country."

She studied him frankly for a long minute and again he was aware of her considerable charm. Even with trouble and doubt in her eyes she was a very pretty woman. Finally she said bluntly, "I'm sorry to sound suspicious but you haven't told me the whole truth about yourself, you know."

He hoped his laugh sounded natural. "All I've told you is that I was once on duty in this part of the country and that I had heard of a man named Trappe. I've hardly had the time or opportunity to give you my life history."

"You said you knew Mr. Hockett. You didn't tell me that you really knew him quite well, that you'd been in this house several times."

He kept his ease with something of an effort. "You've been so busy bossing me around I didn't have any chance to tell you things."

"Don't evade. What I said is true, isn't it?"

"About knowing Hockett? Sure it is. I knew Hockett quite well. I came here hoping to work for him. Smith came along because I told him about the place. But how'd you guess it?"

"You knew your way around. The kitchen sink and pump aren't in sight from the back door but you went to the pump without a bit of hesitation. And you came into the valley across some country where there are no regular trails."

"And I wear cavalry pants," he added with a laugh. "You're quite an observer—Mrs. Kendrick." He managed to get the name out without too much delay.

"And did you know my husband? You never answered that question."

"I knew a corporal in the Third Cavalry who was killed at the Rosebud fight. His name was Tom Kendrick."

"My husband," she said steadily. "He was not killed. At first he was missing and believed dead but he made his way back and was discharged at the end of his enlistment. While his regiment was on another campaign, I understand."

For a moment Kendrick wondered if they were both playing the same game of stating facts in a deceiving manner. Then he saw the honest concern in the dark eyes and decided that the girl believed what she was saying.

"Things like that happened," he agreed. "So I suppose Kendrick hunted up his old sweetheart, married her, and then came out here to join his uncle. I happen to know that Hockett was his uncle, you see."

"Not quite. I came out here with my father when he set up his assay office in Packsaddle. That was two summers ago. I met Tom Kendrick when he first arrived to claim his property last August. We were married in September." Her voice broke a little as she completed the statement.

"You didn't tell me your name, she said after she had taken a moment or two to steady her voice.

"Cavanagh, ma'am," he told her. "Tom Cavanagh." It was his first real lie but there seemed to be no evading it. He picked the Cavanagh part because he was beginning to suspect that the false Kendrick had really been Ed Cavanagh. The "Tom" was a safety measure in case Smith forgot and called him by that name.

He stood up carefully, finding that the wound gave him no great discomfort. Swallowing the last of the coffee he took the cup to the kitchen, rinsed it at the pump and placed it on the table. Then he turned to face the girl who had followed him to the doorway. "I think I'll have a try at tracking those cattle killers," he announced. "I'm getting curious to know what's been going on around here."

"You'd better stay out of it," she warned soberly. "There's no reason for you to risk getting involved."

"Maybe there is, though," he replied. "I kind of owe something to Bill Hockett—and I wouldn't mind putting in a few good licks for Tom Kendrick. Want to tell me what you know about the mess?"

"There's little to tell. I came to Packsaddle with my father just after there was a gold strike on Van Bremer's

57

Creek. It didn't turn out to be a big strike but it brought enough prospectors into the country so that Amos Trappe found it worth his while to move his trading post up here. Meanwhile an English cattle company called the North American Cattle Association had moved into the hills just north of here. They also deal with Trappe. Mostly, though, his business—and the other business of Packsaddle—is with prospectors. The troubles here have been quite mysterious; no one knew who to blame for the raids."

"Until this morning?"

"Of course. I saw those men. They came from the direction of North American's main ranch. Amos—Mr. Trappe, that is—has hinted a number of times that it was cattlemen who were trying to drive off the owners of this homestead but I couldn't believe him. Now I begin to wonder."

"Then it's high time we found out a few things," Kendrick told her grimly. "I'll hit their trail and see where they went. When Smith comes back tell him to follow me; he'll be able to read my sign well enough."

"But you're wounded. One man alone shouldn't . . . "

"I'll take care of myself. Anyway I won't go very far. I just want to check up on a few things. Smith can make sure I don't run into any trouble."

She went to the corner and brought out the rifle he had noticed before. "Take this with you," she said quietly. "My husband said it was an excellent weapon—but maybe you would know about that since it originally belonged to Mr. Hockett."

"I remember it," he told her with a nod. "It's a good one. Thanks."

He went out with the big rifle in his hand, wondering how many odd twists this situation would develop before he could declare himself. Because his thoughts were running off in so many directions it didn't occur to him that he hadn't picked up ammunition for the rifle but the girl was more thoughtful. She hurried out to him as he prepared to mount, holding out a handful of the clumsy looking shells. "You *might* need them," she said with a tight little smile.

"I'm getting stupid," he grinned. "Lucky you're smart enough to make up for both of us." Another thought oc-

58

curred to him. "What about leaving you here alone? Will you be all right?"

"Of course. Packsaddle is only about five miles down the creek. Your friend Smith ought to be heading back by this time. Amos and his butcher crew won't be much behind him and probably my father will come out when he hears of the raid. I'll be safe enough."

That was twice she had referred to Trappe as Amos, Kendrick realized. He wondered what it meant. His own memory of Amos Trappe was not a particularly clear one but the impression was of a sharp trader, a man who had never been too particular about how he got his money. This woman didn't seem like the kind to be friendly with Amos Trappe.

He picked up the trail of the raiders while he was trying to sort out his thoughts. It was easy to follow them across the grassy valley and within a few minutes he was sending his mount up a sloping path much like the one he and Smith had descended. This one angled to the north, however, and presently Kendrick found himself in country which he had never explored. He knew its general nature, of course, but in the rush of homesteading he had never found time for anything but essential labor.

The thought brought its own bitterness. His labor—and Uncle Bill's—largely wasted! He paused long enough to look back across the wide bend of Packsaddle Creek, seeing again the beauty of the little valley he had picked out as his own eight years before. He could almost pick out the boundaries of his own quarter section and that of Uncle Bill. Hockett's had been the Number One Section, Northwest Quarter. Kendrick's was the southwest quarter of the same section and they had usually referred to the joint claim simply as Number One, assuming that the rugged eastern half would never be claimed. It was a pretty spot, all right, freshly green at the bend of the creek, the dark pines framing the open valley. Today, however, it was difficult to think in terms of beauty. Something sinister and ugly had come into the country. Murder had been done. Maybe more murder was planned.

He turned away quickly, going back to the easily

marked tracks of the cattle killers. The four men had halted at the top of the climb and he could see a few blood spots on a rock. Evidently they had stopped here to bandage the man he had nicked. Then they had ridden straight north, traversing a country that was a sort of rough plateau above the creek valley. Some of the land was barren, mostly rock and gravel, but there were some surprising little valleys in which the bunch grass grew lush. Kendrick was not surprised when he began to see small bunches of cattle in these grassy spots. This must be a part of the range that had been taken over by the English company.

He stuck to his tracking for a good five miles, passing one lot of stock so close that he could read the NA brand on the animals. Then the marks merged with a definite trail and he suspected that it might be the same one he had spotted on the previous night. Evidently NA cattle were moved across this plateau to some area farther south and east. The only fresh hoof marks went in that direction.

It seemed useless to track the raiders any farther, now that he had trailed them to NA range, so he turned back, studying the country as he worked toward the valley once more. It seemed pretty certain that he was going to need a lot more information about NA. A big outfit like that wasn't running the usual kind of ranch that appeared up here in the high country. Tracing the raiders to NA was not going to be enough; he wanted to know why the raid had taken place. Particularly a daylight raid.

He met Smith just at the top of the slanting trail and they pulled up to exchange ideas. The butcher's crew was already at work in the valley, Mac reported. Trappe himself had come out and was making romantic remarks to the fair widow.

"Who is she, Tom?" the little man asked. "I didn't dare ask any questions after I saw that something was out of kilter, and I'm getting mighty curious."

"I don't blame you. The lady claims to be Mrs. Tom Kendrick, widow of Uncle Bill's nephew."

"How's that again?"

Kendrick grinned crookedly. "You heard right. Apparently my uncle was killed in some kind of a raid early last summer, maybe a raid like the one we interrupted this morning. His nephew, Corporal Tom Kendrick of the Third Cavalry, falsely reported killed in action at the Rosebud, showed up and claimed the property. There was no mention of any objections being raised so I guess he made good on the claim. He also married a girl who had recently moved into the region. They seem to have lived in the cabin over the winter but then another raid took place and the man was killed. So the lady claims to be the widow of Tom Kendrick."

"You think she's in on the swindle?"

"Somehow I don't. I didn't want to ask too many questions but I'm guessing the fellow fooled her in the same way he must have fooled the local authorities."

"Can you prove the truth of it?"

"I suppose so. But it might be smart to let things ride for a while. Somebody seems to want this place real bad. They've already killed two men. Now they're trying to scare the girl away. If I declare myself, I'm ripe for bullets—without even knowing what the shooting's all about. If I wait to see how the swindle was worked I may be in a better position to face the big fight."

"What about this man Trappe? Did he know you?"

"That's a point that bothers me. I only remember him vaguely. I imagine he won't remember me. I was just another trooper who used to pass his place. Maybe the man who pretended to be Kendrick could have fooled Amos Trappe; maybe he played his game with Trappe's help."

Smith whistled. "That's a point. Got any idea who worked the game?"

"Some. I'm picking Ed Cavanagh as my number-one suspect. Ed knew how things shaped up here. He about fits my description. He could have fooled people like the county land agent who never saw me but once. But he couldn't have fooled Amos Trappe. Ed and Amos were pretty thick for a while."

"Sounds possible. Ed left the army—and he wasn't expecting to. I'd guess he came back from the Rosebud with the detachment of wounded—including me—and found the letter about your uncle's death. He thought you were dead so he figured nobody else would know the difference. Trappe would have been the only one who could catch him on it, and you say Trappe was a friend of his."

"That's how it looks to me. I think Ed came here and claimed the property, and Trappe helped him do it. But what about the letter I wrote? Did it ever come through? Did Ed know I'd turned up alive? Does Trappe know it?"

"How d'you figure to find out?"

Kendrick frowned. "I guess we've got to make some opening moves. Let's get down there and talk to Amos."

8

THEY descended to the valley before either of them spoke again. Then it was Smith who held up a warning hand as they struck the level ground with its screen of pines. "Let me get a couple of things straight, Tom. What's the game if Trappe recognizes you?"

Kendrick shrugged. "Then I play the hand face up. I came here to claim what's mine. I don't propose to be turned aside either by thieves trying to scare their way into control or by swindlers trying to get control in some other way."

"Do you figure he'll be looking for you to show up? Trappe, I mean?"

"I don't know about that. Watch him close when we first meet and I'll pretend I'm not much interested in him. I don't think he'd recognize me unless something jogged his memory pretty hard—and maybe not even then."

"What am I supposed to look for?"

"Signs of recognition, even interest. I wrote a letter to Uncle Bill, remember. Somebody must have got that letter. Somebody knows I'm still alive. I wonder if it's Amos Trappe."

"Right. I'll watch."

"And keep an eye out for some reaction to the name I gave the lady. I told her I was Tom Cavanagh."

"That's a good one! If Cavanagh is the one who came down here and made some kind of deal with Trappe the name ought to stir up some kind of a fuss."

"Maybe that's a good idea. I want to see who makes what kind of fuss."

"A sound Shakespearean strategy," Smith agreed solemnly. "Methinks there's a passage in *Julius Caesar* to the effect that it is better that the enemy seek us, so that he shall waste his means. I won't vouch for the phrasing being exactly correct."

"A bad sign," Kendrick told him. "You haven't sprung a Shakespeare quotation on me in over a month. I hoped you'd reformed."

The little man laughed. " 'Nature her custom holds, Let shame say what it will.' That's from *Hamlet,* in case you're interested."

Kendrick kneed his horse out toward the open valley. "I'll bet you met the girl's old man. She told me her father is a Shakespeare quoter. It sounds like you've been corrupted in a hurry."

"Quite a character, the old fellow is," Smith agreed cheerfully.

"And what about Amos Trappe? Did you meet him?"

"Long enough to pass the lady's message that he should bring a butchering crew out to 'Mrs. Kendrick's.' That's when I began to see we were in a most intriguing situation. I figured you'd made a quick conquest."

"Stop the joking. What did you think of Trappe?"

"Seemed like a smooth article. Acts mighty important —and tries to look the part."

"That's different. I recalled him as being lazy and a bit dirty."

"He's changed. There ought to be a quotation somewhere about how fortune alters the shapes of men but I can't think what it is."

"Good. I'm having enough trouble thinking straight about real things without getting the bard mixed up in it."

"What about the lady?" Smith suggested. "You're Tom

Kendrick and she's Mrs. Tom Kendrick. It could be an interesting point."

"Don't talk like an idiot!"

"You might do worse. She's quite a gal."

"And maybe party to a fraud. If she isn't—how is she going to feel about me when I spring the truth on her?"

They rode on to the cabin and dismounted, Kendrick getting a twinge in his side but paying scant attention to it. He was more concerned with the complexities of this situation.

Three people came out to greet them, the girl and two men. One of the strangers was a big fellow, as tall as Kendrick and considerably broader. He seemed to match the combined memory and description of Amos Trappe and Kendrick threw him a cool but searching glance. Trappe looked prosperous. He wore well tailored Eastern clothing that still had an air of the West about it and his ruddy features were clean shaven except for a flowing mustache. The other man was shorter, older, and white haired, suggesting a frontier Santa Claus in his roundness and general air of good humor. If he was at all worried over the attack on the homestead he didn't show it.

"Did you learn anything?" the girl asked abruptly.

Kendrick nodded, deliberately avoiding any further glance at Trappe. "A little. The raiders climbed to that high country over in the northeast and then rode straight north. I trailed them about four miles, I'd guess. They must have been headed toward this new cattle outfit you mentioned. At any rate their trail got all fouled up with cattle tracks. Quite a few head of stock up there."

"Oh, dear!" the girl shook her head unhappily. "I was afraid it would be that way. Those men this morning looked like some of the NA riders I've seen passing here but I couldn't believe that Mr. Craddock would permit such a thing to happen."

"I'll take care of it, my dear," Trappe said. "Craddock probably doesn't know about it. Between us we'll smoke 'em out."

"But why are they doing it? Can they be the same ones who killed Tom and Mr. Hockett?"

"Don't worry any more about it. I'll take care of everything. If it's Craddock's men at the bottom of this outrage we'll get matters under control in a hurry." There was no mistaking the protective note in his voice.

Kendrick had a feeling the girl didn't like to hear him talk like that. She looked around a little worriedly and her eye caught the patch of blood at Kendrick's side. Instantly she became solicitous. "You're bleeding again, Mr. Cavanagh. Get into the house so I can attend to it. I knew you had no business riding so soon."

Kendrick obeyed meekly enough, the girl adding off-hand introductions as they went back into the cabin. Kendrick's nose told him that her father had been drinking. Probably that accounted for his rubicund good humor.

Trappe stood by while the girl replaced the dressing on Kendrick's wound, his frown hinting that he was not pleased with the way things were going. Still he sounded casual as he commented, "Mrs. Kendrick tells me you men used to know Bill Hockett."

"Not Smith. Just me," Kendrick said, not even looking up. "I was on patrol duty down this way about six years ago. I was over here a couple of times to lend a hand with some of the building."

"Then you knew Kendrick?"

"Sure did."

"Do I understand your name is Cavanagh?"

"Yep."

"Ed Cavanagh?"

"Tom. Ed was in the same outfit as Kendrick. I used to get mixed up a bit with Ed because we looked a bit alike—only he had a mustache. No relation, though."

"I never could see it," Smith put in. "You and Ed might've been about the same build but that was all."

"What happened to Ed?" Trappe asked, his tone sharpening just a trifle.

Kendrick looked up for the first time. "Come to think of it, I don't believe I ever heard. After that dust-up on the Rosebud our outfit was separated from L troop. I heard that Kendrick got killed but I didn't hear any report on Ed Cavanagh."

"I explained about the false death report," the girl said quietly.

65

"That's why we headed down this way," Smith said, taking over the talk. "Tom knew about this place and we got to thinking that maybe this man Hockett could use some hired hands, being as how his nephew wouldn't be coming back to join him. Leaves a man all at sea to find his figuring was wrong on so many counts. It was mighty tough on poor Kendrick to pull out of that mess on the Rosebud and then come down here to get himself killed by cattle raiders." He looked around at the girl and added, "Sorry, ma'am. I didn't mean to mention it; I'm just a little confused all around."

"So are we all of us," the little round man said in a surprisingly deep voice. "More puzzled than the Egyptians in their fog. That's from *Twelfth Night,* by the way."

"Don't quote, father," the girl said quickly. "I'm in no mood for maudlin literary flourishes."

"Maudlin, indeed!" The little man seemed quite outraged. "I drink no more than will do me good." He nodded briskly toward Kendrick and confided, "That is a quotation also, my friend."

Smith chuckled. *"Henry the Fourth,* I believe. There's another from *Twelfth Night* which goes, 'That quaffing and drinking will undo you.' "

The girl had frowned at Smith's intervention but now she suddenly relaxed a little and laughed. "Thank you, Mr. Smith," she exclaimed. "I'm glad someone can give him a dose of his own medicine."

"I bow to you, sir," the round man said, suiting the gesture to the word. "You are a scholar, sir. To quote the same *Henry the Fourth,* 'For my part, I speak it to my shame, I have a truant been.' "

"Let me get in the game," Kendrick said suddenly. "Didn't I see one somewhere about somebody being 'fat-witted with drinking old sack'?"

"That's Father," the girl said quickly.

"I've got to head back to town," Amos Trappe broke in. "When everybody gets done talking nonsense come in and we'll try to figure out some way to get things straightened out." He looked straight at the girl and added, "Of course, you know, there's one way to do it without any more trouble. I shall be at your service."

He went out without bothering to offer any comment to any of the others.

Kendrick broke the awkward silence that followed Trappe's departure. "Would I be prying too much if I asked what makes him sound like he's got the answer to this problem?"

"No reason why you shouldn't know," the girl said with a shrug.

"Mr. Trappe and I are partners," her father stated with firm dignity.

"Partners, eh?" Kendrick commented. "Partners in this homestead?"

"I'd better explain it all," the girl said with a small frown. "Father met Mr. Trappe when we first came out to this country. There was talk about moving the old trading post up here into the hills so as to be better located for taking care of the business with the prospectors who had started pouring in. Amos needed extra capital for building the new place. Father had money to invest. It seemed like a good way to buy into a profitable business and at the same time start a new town where an assay office might be set up."

"But the partnership doesn't extend to this place here?"

"Not exactly. My husband made a lot of improvements after he took over the place—and most of those improvements were made with materials supplied on credit by Mr. Trappe. Until those debts are paid off it's obvious that Mr. Trappe has an interest."

"That still doesn't explain his hint that he could get around the trouble that's been nagging you."

She flushed a little but still gave a steady answer. "When we first came out here Mr. Trappe was very attentive to me. He asked me to marry him. I didn't exactly turn him down but I did put him off. Then Tom Kendrick arrived and things seemed different to me. I married Tom. That seemed to end it for Amos Trappe but since Tom's death Amos *has* been passing some very broad hints."

"Sensible hints," her father interrupted. "Jo can't handle this place alone—even if the outlaws let her alone. If she married Amos she could sell this farm and have nothing to worry about."

67

"My husband has been dead less than three months," she said firmly but with some show of spirit. "I'll not talk of marriage. Anyway I like this place and I don't propose to let a band of thugs drive me away!"

Her father shrugged and turned aside as though unwilling to get involved in an old argument which had been repeated many times before. Kendrick could appreciate her sentiments, mostly because they were practically his own. Still there didn't seem to be anything more for him to say.

Smith took it from there. "Sounds like another partnership deal might be a smart idea. Tom and I have a bit of capital—and we're used to risks. You supply the land and let us work it."

"No," she said flatly. "The danger is mine; I can't ask strangers to share it."

"You didn't ask," Smith pointed out. "I did. We need a place to settle. You need help. We'll put it all in writing."

"Maybe . . ."

Smith laughed aloud. "She's set to agree, gents. As they say in *Two Gentlemen of Verona,* 'a woman sometimes scorns what best contents her.' Is it a deal, ma'am?"

Everyone laughed at the impudence of it, Kendrick appreciating Smith's cleverness more than the others did. "We'd like it fine, ma'am," he said, meaning it. Any reasonable kind of excuse for remaining in the valley was good for something. It might keep the girl from going to Trappe and his offer of assistance—and there was one obvious way to make sure that she did not suffer from the deception. A partnership with a pretty woman like this one suggested many pleasant ideas. . . .

"I'm hungry," he said. "Let's talk business over the supper table. Do we get invited?"

Now the strain was completely gone, everyone making suggestions at the same time. Within minutes they untangled some of the ideas and the girl turned her hand to supper preparations, drafting her father as assistant while Smith and Kendrick went over to Kendrick's own cabin to make it habitable for the night. The place had never really been used, having been constructed mostly to meet the building requirements of the Homestead Act.

68

However, it was solidly built and would serve the immediate purpose perfectly.

The interval gave the two men a chance to compare notes and Kendrick found that Smith agreed with him on most of the guesses he had been making. Trappe was trying hard to get the widow to marry him. Whether he really wanted her or the property was something yet to be determined. It wasn't unlikely that he was interested in both.

"We've got two lines of investigation to follow," Kendrick summed it up. "I want to know who killed Uncle Bill and why? If we get the answer to the why of it we'll probably know the whole story. Then we can figure out who we need to fight."

"Any doubt about it being the cattle outfit?"

"Maybe. I feel pretty sure that somebody from NA staged this morning's raid—but I'm not sure it means a war between cattleman and farmer. The stake just isn't big enough. A daylight raid on top of two killings has to have something pretty important behind it."

"Sounds likely. Your second point is about Ed Cavanagh, I suppose?"

"Right. I want to know whether his widow had any hint of the truth. First, though, I want to be sure it was Cavanagh."

"Does it make any difference?"

"Some. If it was Ed, then Trappe knew the truth. If somebody else passed himself off as me it's possible that Trappe didn't know."

"Think he has any suspicion about you now?"

"You answer that. You were supposed to be watching him."

"I think he's fooled. Probably he's convinced that Tom Kendrick is dead."

"Dead in Wyoming or dead here?"

Smith shook his head. "That's one we've got to find out about. Any idea how to do it?"

"Some. I'd like to see the personal effects left by the man who was killed here. If any of my stuff shows up in the lot it'll be a good bet that Cavanagh brought them here. Nobody else would have been likely to have a chance at them."

"And what happens if we figure it was Ed?"
"We'll see when the time comes."

9

THE evening turned out to be a good one on all counts, Smith proving himself to be a smooth performer at the business of making everyone feel easy in what might have been an awkward, troubled situation. He carried the burden of the business discussion and at the same time kept them amused with his half-apologetic Shakespearean references. It turned out that the chubby man bore the name of Montgomery Glass and he admitted rather ruefully that he was usually known by his first two initials "M. T." Smith became his firm friend in the first half hour, partly by swapping quotations with him and partly by avoiding the pun on the initials and calling him Monty.

The girl seemed to lose some of her troubled air as the time went along and several times met Kendrick's eyes with something like amused understanding. She seemed happy to have the opportunity to enjoy the levity and Kendrick was well pleased to feel that he shared the amusement with her.

Out of the rattle of loose talk he began to see a sharp picture of what had transpired here along the Packsaddle Creek. Uncle Bill Hockett had been killed in July of 'seventy-six. Raiders had tried to burn his cabin during the night, piling dry brush along the walls. Hockett had apparently run out to stop them and had been shot down at once. The killers had fled without even going through with their arson plans and Hockett's body had been discovered two days later by a prospector coming east out of the hills.

There had been only a superficial investigation by a lawman from Cimarron but the report had been enough so that the federal land agent had recorded the death and sent word of it to Corporal Tom Kendrick, next of kin.

Kendrick—the false one, of course—had turned up at the town of Packsaddle in late August, establishing his claim to the estate without difficulty. The title had been uncontested and the claimant had been doubly successful in also winning the hand of the only unattached young woman in the valley. Joanne Glass had married him less than a month after he arrived in town and the pair had moved into the cabin that had been Bill Hockett's.

Pop Glass had stuck to his assay office in town during the winter, the newlyweds spending a busy three months in preparing the place for the big plans they were making. The cabin had been given the improvements which Kendrick had already noted and they had been about to start work on a stable and some new corrals when the raiders struck again, this time working silently and cutting the throats of eight head of stock during the night. A week later they made another raid—but this time the man calling himself Kendrick had heard them. He went out to beat off the attack and was killed just as Hockett had been.

By the time the talk came around to that point the air of jollity had disappeared. Two murders and the certainty that the killers were still operating left no room for joking. Kendrick decided to risk a question or two.

"We'll have to plan some way to stop them," he said quietly. "That means we've got to find out what they mean by these raids. Somebody is mighty anxious to get hold of this property. What can be so valuable about three hundred acres of hay meadow and fair-to-middling farm land?"

"NA is rather short of hay land, I understand," the girl said. "But would they go to such extremes for that?"

"You didn't seem to think so a while ago," Kendrick told her. "You hinted that you thought their foreman was a pretty decent sort."

"I met him a couple of times and he seemed that way. He'd made an agreement with Mr. Hockett to permit NA cattle to be moved across this land by the far side of the creek. After my husband and I came here to live he stopped by to ask if we proposed to continue the agreement. We had no objection and my impression was that

71

he wanted to get along with us. That's why I don't understand any of this."

"Has NA used that trail for drives since you've been here?"

"Several times. They took a big bunch of Texas cattle up the creek early last winter and twice that I recall they've brought down fatted stock for sale to Amos Trappe. There was never any trouble at all."

Kendrick caught Smith's swift glance but said nothing. That cattle trail in the high country was a matter he preferred not to discuss just yet. Why was it there when NA had an easier route?

"Anything else that might mean value to anybody?" he persisted. "Did any of these wandering prospectors ever get interested around here?"

Mr. Glass answered that one. "I'm sure they didn't. My assay office is a pretty good place to keep tabs on mineral strikes. After the finds on Van Bremer's Creek there were prospectors poking around everywhere. Nobody ever hinted that there was color within twenty-five miles of here."

"Did your husband ever say anything that would lead you to believe he had any ideas on the subject?" Kendrick asked the girl.

"Never. He tried to find out who killed his uncle but he never got an inkling. Or I don't know about it if he did."

"Have you looked over his papers?" Smith cut in. "Maybe there'd be some clue in the title papers that would suggest some value to the place that isn't generally known."

She shook her head. "I've never even looked at them. Mr. Trappe has been warning me that I ought to take the proper legal steps to get the title in my own name but I haven't had the heart to make the effort. I really don't know what is in the papers."

"Why not get them out, Jo?" her father suggested. "It's only fair to your new partners that they have all the help they can get in this matter."

She assented willingly enough and went into the other room to pull a wooden box from under the bunk. Ken-

72

drick went to help her and presently they were running through an assortment of documents which immediately answered one question. Ed Cavanagh had certainly been the man who had pretended to be Tom Kendrick. Everything Kendrick had left behind at Fort Fetterman was here in the lot. No one but Cavanagh would have been able to get his hands on these letters and personal papers.

Kendrick didn't dare glance at Smith. He knew what the little man would be thinking. Cavanagh had seized what looked like a good opportunity to improve his situation without undue risk. There would be no one to know the difference except Amos Trappe. It meant that Trappe was involved. Jo Glass and her father had been drawn into the tangle without having any idea what deception was included in it.

On the other matter the papers told nothing. Cavanagh had simply taken the legal steps the real Kendrick would have taken, getting a good title to the property. There was the original homestead deed in the name of Thomas Kendrick and a territorial deed giving Kendrick title to the strip he had described to Smith as the Spanish strip. Both documents, Kendrick knew, had been left in Uncle Bill's care so it was natural that they were here now. The third paper of importance was the one in which Thomas Kendrick was certified as the owner of inheritance of the homestead rights of William Hockett, deceased. Everything was in order and there was no hint as to why anyone should be trying to drive off the owner of this particular bit of property.

One item of interest was not in the collection—the letter Kendrick had written to Bill Hockett after returning to Fort Fetterman. With Packsaddle now a town of some consequence it seemed certain that such a letter would have been delivered. But to whom? Uncle Bill was dead by that time. Had Cavanagh received it and kept it a secret? Or did Trappe know about it?

The two men excused themselves after the examination of the papers, moving back across the valley to their new bunk house in the soft gloom of a fine spring evening. The talk had died away when it became apparent that nothing was to be learned from the legal documents.

73

Well out of earshot of the cabin, Smith asked, "Cavanagh, was it?"

"It had to be. If Ed had charge of cleaning up the effects of the casualties he'd be the only one who could have laid his hands on some of the things she has there. I saw them last at Fort Fetterman."

"The dirty crook!"

"Don't be hard on him. He thought I was dead. There was no one else with any claim. It was fraud, all right, but there was nothing personal in it. Ed wasn't doing anything to hurt me."

"Well . . . maybe not."

"Perhaps he even helped. The papers transfer the Hockett property to Tom Kendrick. That's me. I can claim the benefit of the legal routines Ed went through. Maybe it saved me a lot of red tape. If the state had seized the property for lack of an heir I might have had plenty of trouble. Anyway, Ed didn't have much luck. It was Ed who got killed, not me."

"You've got a point there. But what happens when his widow starts to put in her claim for a new transfer of title? You'll have to make some kind of move then."

"Time enough for that when it happens. We've got other things to do first. Tomorrow morning I want you to head into Packsaddle and buy the tools we'll need to work this place. While you're there make some inquiries of the post office, if they have one. Take my discharge papers and the other things they sent me in clearing up my case. Just show the postmaster the part where it says 'in the matter of Thomas Kendrick, reported killed-in-action' and hint that you're an agent of the army trying to close out the matter. You're just the fellow to get away with the act. What I really want to know is whether an army notice regarding my death was ever received here—and whether my letter of last fall ever was delivered. While you're at it keep your ear tuned for gossip."

"And what are you aiming to do?"

"I'm going to make NA a visit. Either that outfit's our enemy or it isn't. I want to find out."

Next morning they discussed their plans in some detail while they looked over the place, deciding what kind of tools and equipment would have to be bought. Then they went over to the main cabin and had breakfast with Monty Glass and Jo. She was to provide meals as part of the partnership arrangement.

It was the girl who brought up the subject they had been discussing on the previous evening. "Maybe I was wrong about one thing last night," she said as the meal was over. "Perhaps my husband suspected something that he didn't tell me about. It was all rather vague but I recall that he came home from Packsaddle one day looking pretty glum. Right after that he began to talk about selling out to NA and moving farther west. He wouldn't say why."

"But he did mention NA?"

"That's right."

"Did he talk to anyone from there about a deal?"

"Not after that, I'm sure. We were winter-bound for quite a while and he said no more about it." Her voice broke a little as she added, "It was when winter broke that he was killed."

Later, while he was helping Smith at some of the chores Kendrick murmured, "Looks like Ed got the letter I wrote to reassure Uncle Bill. Somebody caught up with him before he could make his move."

"Think he knew who was doing it?"

"Hard to say. Maybe he just knew that his game was up so far as I was concerned. He figured I wouldn't get down here until after the snow was gone and his delay killed him. That means he got it in my place. Before I let the world know that I'm Kendrick I want to find out who was so anxious to get rid of me."

"Expect to learn anything at NA?"

"Who knows? One way or another I want to find out why there's a cattle trail in the high country when NA has a deal to run cattle along the creek. It's as good a puzzle to start on as any."

Smith laughed shortly. "You've sure got plenty of choice in puzzles."

Twenty minutes later Smith, Glass and the girl headed down the creek toward Packsaddle while Kendrick sent his horse up the steep slope which the raiders had used on the previous morning. He found the craglands silent except for the birds so he cut sharply toward the east instead of following the sign he had checked before. This time he was interested in another trail, the one he had seen before reaching the valley.

He found it easily enough, noting that there was no sign along it. The last herd to pass there had been a small one headed southeast. The marks were a good week old.

He traveled with extreme caution as he backtracked, judging that the men who had killed Hockett and Cavanagh were probably interested in this trail. Maybe they wouldn't know that it was the real Tom Kendrick who was now investigating it but he had to assume that they would shoot first and make their identifications later.

He covered five miles with no sign of life but then he found himself in the same succession of little draws he had noticed closer to the valley rim. Evidently this broken country stretched out for some distance and the English syndicate had picked it for cattle range because it had good patches of grass. Along with the upper reaches of the creek valley it would form a fine big ranch. That was what was needed here; it took a lot of acreage to support a cow in this country.

Because he was keeping to the scant cover of the high country's scrub junipers he moved more slowly as he advanced, searching out each little valley before showing himself on its rim. After a while that caution paid off. About a mile to the south, coming up behind him on the mysterious trail, he spotted a rider.

By that time there was no well defined cattle trail but only the marks of grazing animals spread over a wide area. The trail to the south was clearly one of small herds that had been rounded up in this part of the high country and hazed southward through the craglands. Kendrick studied the approaching rider briefly and then moved into the best available bit of cover and dismounted. He wanted to know who it was who was following the mysterious trail but he hoped the man wouldn't ride too close to him. Junipers didn't grow very high up here.

Minutes later he recognized the oncoming rider as Amos Trappe. The big trader passed without seeing the hidden watcher and Kendrick let him cross the next low rise before mounting to follow. Maybe this trip was going to turn out interesting in a manner not foreseen.

It was no great trick to keep the unsuspecting Trappe in sight. Kendrick's scouting tactics had been learned in a dozen Indian campaigns. About a mile to the north he saw Trappe meet two men who rode out of a brushy draw. At the distance he could tell little about them except that one wore a bright blue shirt.

He swung to the left, leading his pony and following the south slope of a ridge so that he could peer across it and watch the meeting without being seen by the distant trio. The move quickly took him to a sharp drop which he guessed was the edge of the crag country. There he halted and watched, aware that Trappe was doing a lot of violent talking. The other men seemed uneasy, perhaps a bit evasive, but Trappe was certainly stating his case in strong terms.

The confab lasted several minutes and then Trappe turned his horse and came back over the same path he had covered in heading north. The other pair conferred for several minutes; then the blue shirted rider rode away to the north while the other man went back into the draw.

Kendrick waited until Trappe passed the spot where he was concealed. Then he remounted and headed down the steep slope to the west, partly because the pines gave him better cover and partly because he knew that the creek was down there. NA could not be much farther away and it seemed like a good idea to approach the place from a normal quarter. It was going to be interesting to learn whether a man in a bright blue shirt would show up at the ranch.

He reached the creek bottom rather quickly, realizing that the difference in elevation between valley and plateau was less than it was opposite the Hockett cabin. There was a well marked trail along the stream, obviously the one NA used in going back and forth to Packsaddle. The valley was narrow at that particular point but within a half mile it widened quickly and he found a valley much like the one he knew so well. He guessed that he was now only about a dozen miles away from his own property but he had never seen this piece of land before. In the old days he had never found time for more than the essential chores of getting his property organized. Army leaves had not given him any time for exploring.

NA cattle were all along the creek and he decided that this part of the syndicate's range was reserved for their better breeds of stock. The upland was good enough for the ordinary run but down here they had some pretty fancy beef. It appeared that NA had organized with some intelligence.

He rounded a bend of the creek valley and saw the cluster of buildings and corrals which marked the outfit's headquarters. Everything looked permanent and substantial. Certainly this was a big company, scarcely the kind of crowd that would be expected to go in for vicious attacks on neighbors.

There were men working near one of the big new corrals while a calf branding crew could be seen at their task along the base of the far ridge. Nobody seemed to notice the stranger until he was within two hundred yards of the ranch house. Then two men came out of a wagon shed, one of them wearing a bright blue shirt. Kendrick saw that they were eyeing him but he could not guess whether they recognized him or not. On his side there could be no doubt; the little man with the bald head was certainly the scrawny little rider who had led the raid against the Hockett cattle. Almost as certainly the blue shirted one was one of the pair who had not come close enough to Kendrick to exchange shots in the brief skirmish. Without doubt he was the man who had talked to Amos Trappe on the plateau.

The bald man said something to his companion and blue shirt went back behind the shed again. Then the little man took a couple of steps forward as though anxious to challenge the newcomer.

"No grub-line riders wanted," he growled as Kendrick came within ear-shot. "Better hit on back the way you come." His bald head shone pink in the morning sunshine but there was a malignity in his narrow features which belied the cherubic pink of his head. Kendrick had a feeling that he'd seen that face and head before—

and it hadn't been on the previous morning. At that time a big hat had concealed those notable features. The memory of that scowling face was something that went back much farther.

10

"You the boss around here?" Kendrick inquired mildly. "I'm not looking for a job, if that's what's worrying you."

"Then state yer business!" The words were almost a snarl as the thin man crouched slightly. Here was another of those chip-shouldered little gents, Kendrick thought, a small man who thought he had to make himself look big by acting belligerent—especially with a gun.

"I want to talk about a business matter with the boss of this outfit. His name is Craddock, I believe. If you're Craddock just say so." He made it sound pretty cool as he tried to size up the man in front of him. Somehow he didn't think that the bald man had recognized him. The fellow was simply being his own nasty self. Probably he didn't realize he was talking to a man with whom he had recently exchanged bullets.

For a moment or two he thought the bald man might make some sort of hostile move but then the tension was broken as a mild voice spoke from a window of the ranch house. "Over this way, cowboy. I'm Craddock."

The little man stiffened but then turned away, muttering under his breath. It seemed clear that he resented his boss almost as much as he did the calm stranger. Still he was not ready to start anything just now.

Kendrick kneed his mount across to the hitch rack which ran along the broad veranda of the ranch house. A stoutish, fair-haired man of about forty came out of the house, his slight frown more questioning than disagreeable. He had a pale complexion which made his blond hair and mustache seem all the more colorless, pale eyes adding to a sort of faded youthfulness.

79

"Don't mind Baldy," he greeted. "He gets sullen at times." His voice held a high-pitched British accent. Apparently the syndicate had sent one of their own people over to run this American venture.

"You Mr. Craddock?" Kendrick asked, dismounting.

"I am. You spoke of business?"

"A small matter, I suppose. My name's Cavanagh. It happens I'm considering a sort of partnership arrangement in the homestead claim between here and Packsaddle, the property you probably know as the Hockett-Kendrick place. There's talk of some kind of trouble between you people and the homestead folks. It seemed like a good idea to find out about such a thing before getting myself involved."

The Englishman's face clouded. "I'll offer you some good advice," he snapped. "Stay clear of that aggregation!"

"Then there is really trouble?"

"There is. And it will get worse unless the law takes a hand to keep that thieving assortment of rascals from stealing our cattle!"

"Now I'm hearing something different," Kendrick said as calmly as he could manage. "Do you mind explaining what you mean?"

"Not in the least." The blond man's tone was bitter. "When we moved into this country I thought we had an honest neighbor. Hockett, I mean. We tried to treat him fairly—and for a long time I believed that he was as honest as he seemed. Now I know that he must have been a front man for a blasted gang of cattle thieves. I don't know who was in the band but Hockett was certainly their agent if not their actual leader."

Again Kendrick had to force himself into a show of calmness. "That won't square with the story I've been hearing," he said. "Hockett was killed by raiders who tried to burn him out. Later, on a similar raid, this man called Kendrick got the same dose. Yesterday there was another raid, staged by riders who came from somewhere up this way. Are you sure of your facts?"

Craddock's scowl focussed on Kendrick. "What are

you trying to say?" he demanded. "Are you hinting that my men did that killing?"

"I'm trying to find out the truth. Maybe your men had a hand in yesterday's affair. It looks like it to me."

"Listen carefully, Cavanagh," the Englishman snapped. "I don't know who you are or what kind of pretty story you're trying to make me believe—but I do know this. I've stood all the dirty work I propose to stand from that band of thugs down the creek. I assume Hockett was killed in a quarrel over the profits of the cattle rustling business. Maybe the other man stepped into something he didn't understand and was killed to keep him quiet. I have a feeling that the young woman who now lives there is not connected with the bandits—but I'm not sure about it. The fact remains that every time there has been trouble around that place we have lost cattle. If you're the honest investor that you claim to be I'd advise you to stay clear of the whole thing. If you're one of the band trying to find out how much I know, I'm warning you that my company has been patient long enough! Any more trouble and we'll take the law into our own hands. It won't be the first time that a cattle company has had to burn out a lot of thieves who pretended to be honest farmers, I assure you."

Kendrick saw that it was hardly the time to argue with the man. Craddock had let his anger rise while he snapped out the ultimatum and now was finding it difficult to restrain his temper. Still it was important that a reply should be made. "You're making a lot of poor guesses, Mr. Craddock. You're naming the wrong people as thieves. Wait until . . . "

A harsh voice broke in behind him. "Sorry to interrupt, boss, but you oughta hear this right away." It was the bald man, his eyes carefully avoiding Kendrick. "Dusty just rode down from the upper line camp to tell me that rustlers hit 'em durin' the night. Dave Neal got a slug in his arm but it ain't bad. They drove off the polecats without losin' no stock."

"Where's Dusty now?" Craddock asked.

"At the wagon shed."

81

"Send him back right away. We'll send a couple extra men up there with them for a while."

He swung to face Kendrick. "You heard that, Cavanagh. I guess that tells its own story, doesn't it?"

Kendrick shook his head. "Maybe not. Is this man Neal a burly sort of fellow with a lot of whiskers?"

"Yes. Why?"

"Then somebody is lying about how he got shot. He took a slug yesterday when he was shooting Hockett cattle down the valley. Maybe you'd better look for your thieves among your own men."

For a moment Kendrick thought the bald man would go for his gun. Craddock intervened swiftly, however, his voice hard as he replied, "I believe my own men. Right now I'm not sure what to believe about you. Maybe you'd be well advised to get out of here before I make up my mind."

He turned on his heel and went into the house, leaving Kendrick to face the sardonic grin of the bald man. Worse than the grin was the light of understanding he could see coming into the close-set eyes. "You heard the boss," Baldy snarled. "Git!" Then he lowered his voice to add, "Next time you decide to act nosey keep your gun handy. You're sure as hell goin' to need it."

"I had it last time," Kendrick reminded him. "Remember?"

The little man didn't bother to respond to that. He turned away and headed toward the wagon shed. Kendrick went back to his horse and swung into the saddle, reluctant to go without making another effort to talk some sense into Craddock but knowing that the effort would be useless. The Englishman had formed his opinion and it wasn't likely that a stranger would be able to influence him, especially a stranger suspected of being an enemy.

As he wheeled his horse he saw the man in the blue shirt riding out from behind the wagon shed and starting up a trail which evidently led to the higher ground. Something in his haste made Kendrick suspicious. Dusty was being sent back to the crag country—but he might have been given other orders than those sent by Craddock.

The ride down the creek was uninterrupted but as

soon as he struck the bend Kendrick cut wide so as to skirt the first slopes of the ridge which occupied most of the Spanish strip. This part of the ridge was probably not on the Kendrick purchase but somehow it seemed good to be there, almost like finding one's self on firm ground after crossing a shaky bridge.

He kept to that section of the valley until he reached the narrows but then he sent his horse up the slope a little, trying for concealment and at the same time for an opportunity to keep the valley under surveillance. This would be the danger spot if Dusty had been sent to prepare an ambush.

Because he was watching the cottonwoods and willows along the creek he almost missed the men on the opposite slope. He had climbed around a bit of projecting rock and the detour brought him to a halt for a moment where he could look back up the valley. That was when he spotted them, two riders coming down from the crags at about the same spot where he had descended an hour earlier. The blue shirt identified Dusty but the other man was unknown. They would strike the creek bottom a good eighth of a mile behind him.

"Looks like I guessed right that time," he muttered to himself. "They can enjoy a nice long wait for me to come along—but I've got to remember that they'll be making another try. Real soon."

In spite of the clear threat to his own safety he was most concerned with the perplexities of the whole situation as he rode on down the creek. It was becoming quite clear that someone was trying to set off NA's boss against the owners of the homestead rights at the lower part of the valley. It was equally clear that the rustling of NA cattle was involved in the matter but Kendrick felt sure that rustling wasn't all of it. No matter how it was figured it didn't add up to enough to warrant the risks somebody had taken.

When he arrived at the Hockett cabin he found his new partners unloading some of their purchases. There was a good farm wagon and a team of sturdy horses that could be used for general farm work. The wagon was well loaded with the hundred and one articles always needed

83

around a farm and Kendrick wondered at the cost. His own meager capital would not have been enough for half of this.

"Faro money," Smith told him with a grin as though reading his mind. "What did you find out up the creek?"

Kendrick told his story in detail, aware that the part about Amos Trappe caused Jo to look very troubled. "It looks to me as if somebody on the NA payroll has been stealing company cattle and using that trail through the crags for the movement of the stolen stock. Perhaps Hockett found out about the trail and they were trying to scare him out of the valley when he put up a fight and was killed."

"What about my husband?" the girl asked swiftly. "I can't believe that he knew anything about such a trail. I'm sure he was never up in the high country during the winter."

"I'm still only guessing," Kendrick told her, "but it could be any of several things. Maybe they wanted to keep this place clear of occupants so no one else would learn the things Hockett must have suspected. Maybe they had already started feeding Craddock that wild yarn about the rustlers being directed from somebody here. In that case they might have been trying to set up more evidence to point toward a quarrel between this imaginary band of thieves they've got him believing in."

"And yesterday's raid?"

He shrugged helplessly. "An attack like that—in broad daylight—is one too much for me. I don't get the idea of it at all."

"One thing," she said quietly, "daylight might have been selected because they knew that I would be alone at that hour. My father usually goes to Packsaddle immediately after breakfast."

"Possible. Got any ideas to account for Amos Trappe making a trip up into the crags today?"

She shook her head. "No. Only that he said he'd put pressure on NA if they were in any way responsible for this dirty business. Maybe he went there to pass the word to that former partner of his who now acts as straw boss for the syndicate."

"Who's that?"

"Floyd Mitchell. He was a sort of partner with Trappe until NA came along. Then he went with them."

Memories began to return. Cavanagh had mentioned Floyd Mitchell that day of the Rosebud fight. Maybe the partnership still existed. Maybe this was the connection between the rustling gang and the additional something which Kendrick knew had to be in the picture.

"Is Mitchell a little bald headed fellow?" he asked.

"Yes."

"He's the one who showed his teeth at me today. He's also the man who led that raid yesterday. Why should Trappe be dealing with him—and by way of a secret trail through the craglands?"

She stared at him for a moment, trouble in the dark eyes. "Are you sure that Amos traveled by the secret trail? You said you were beyond the well defined cattle path when you first saw him behind you."

"Right. Maybe I'm jumping at conclusions. He could have come up from Packsaddle along the rim. But why didn't he ride up the creek along the regular trail?"

"I don't know," she said tersely. "But I shall ask him —soon."

"I'll be interested to hear his story. Meanwhile we'll have to make plans to defend the place. If those fellows up the creek were so anxious to ambush me this afternoon they'll probably try to take a crack at me down here. And I don't think they'll delay long in doing it."

"Another one of those night raids?" she asked, remembered horror clear in her eyes.

"Could be. I imagine we'd be smart to stick together at night. With the four of us in one cabin we could always keep a guard on duty."

She nodded. "That makes sense. Suppose we start by getting you off to bed right now. You look exhausted."

"I feel that way. Wears a man out to be favoring a busted rib all the time. You'd better have the picket take post near the corral. Wake me up when it's my time to take over."

"You'll get your share of duty," she promised. "Now climb into that bunk!"

He could hear them settling details after he had pulled a blanket over him but then he dropped off to sleep, content to feel that he had good allies. Even Mr. Glass sounded determined.

Only an instant later—or so it seemed—he was awakened by a hand on his shoulder, Jo's cautious tones telling him that it was his turn to go on watch. "All quiet so far," she reported. "There's coffee on the stove. I'll not strike a light if you can manage in the dark." She kept a hand on his arm to guide him to the kitchen.

"You just coming off duty?" he asked.

"No. I had my turn just after Father. Smith has been on for the past three hours. I couldn't sleep. Too much to think about."

"Wondering whether you ought to marry Amos?"

He could hear the quick intake of breath and he wondered why he'd asked the question like that.

"That's a peculiar remark for you to make, Mr. Cavanagh," she said after a pause.

"I'm a peculiar fellow."

"So I've noticed. You seem as determined to fight this battle for the valley as though . . . as though you owned it."

He was glad she couldn't see his face but he was sorry he couldn't see hers. Was it possible that she suspected something?

"I'm sorry I said that," she added hastily. "I appreciate what you are doing and I've no call to make that kind of remark."

"To a partner," he said.

Her little laugh was not very confident. "To a partner," she agreed.

"Then, as a partner, I'm interested in having things work out the way I want them to. I don't trust Amos Trappe."

"Why not?"

"Maybe I'm jealous. I have a very attractive woman for a partner, after all."

"Please! There'll be none of that. This is business."

"All right. But Amos Trappe isn't blind—and neither

86

am I. He'll not like the idea of this partnership. Maybe he has more than one reason to dislike it."

"You'd better relieve Smith," she said firmly.

11

STARS twinkled brilliantly in a moonless sky when he slipped out of the back door and moved silently toward the corral. On either side of the valley he could make out the faint outline of the hills, the ridges forming a darker silhouette against the star-studded blackness that was the sky. There was no stirring of breeze, only the crispness of a spring night.

He shivered a little, stretching himself cautiously to test sore ribs and to start a bit of circulation. Far up the valley a coyote yapped faintly and he found himself listening with quick suspicion. Old habits had a way of sticking with a man. In the army a fellow did not live to become a veteran if he failed to become suspicious about such things. All too often the innocent sounds of the night turned out to be the attack signals of hostile Indians.

A shadow stirred into sluggish motion by the corner of the corral and Kendrick moved toward it silently, speaking only when he could use a whisper.

"Any signs of trouble, Mac?"

The little man grumbled a negative. "Not unless you count coyotes," he added. "I reckon these must be real ones. It's not Indians we've got to look out for in this tussle."

"I was just thinking the same thing," Kendrick admitted. "I guess we learned our army lessons pretty good."

"How use doth breed a habit in a man," Mac intoned, his whisper seeming to carry just a trace of the stilted quality so characteristic of the dramatic quotation. "Sorry to spring one on you at this time of night but it was a neat fit. From *Two Gentlemen of Verona,* I think."

"I'll take your word for it. Go get some sleep."

87

"One thing I forgot to tell you before. I didn't get a chance when you first showed up this afternoon. I played games with the postmaster in Packsaddle and he's practically sworn to secrecy as a fellow agent of the good old U.S. government."

"You didn't make him suspicious, I hope."

"Not where it counts. He took one look at that paper I flashed on him and right away he was impressed. A confidential matter about a pension for the departed Tom Kendrick, I let him think. Anyway he told me there never was any mail for Bill Hockett—no time since the post office opened. That's almost a year and a half now."

"Then Uncle Bill didn't get any notice from the army about the Rosebud casualty business?"

"Nope. It looks like Cavanagh held back the official notice and came down here himself—just as we figured it."

"But what happened to my letter?"

"Ed got it. When I said there was never any mail for Hockett I meant there was none he ever received. A letter came for him last fall or winter; the post office man wasn't just sure. He only remembered that he delivered it to Hockett's heir. That must have been when Ed started to worry."

"Right. Now we can concentrate on the rest of the puzzle."

Mac handed over the Navy Springfield. "Here's the cannon. Maybe you can use it in the business before long."

As he swung away to head for the cabin Kendrick had a feeling that it wasn't going to be so easy. The men who had attacked the cabin before were now warned. They would know that Kendrick had out-guessed them in avoiding the ambush in the upper valley so they would assume that he would be taking other precautions. It wasn't likely that they would make a rash attack.

The remaining hours of darkness went by rapidly and a little after daybreak Mr. Glass came out of the cabin, looking like an elderly gnome with his white hair rumpled above his round red face. He brought a cup of coffee for Kendrick.

"Drink it here or go on in for another nap," he suggested cheerfully. "I'll stand guard for a while—if you think it's any longer necessary."

"No use, I imagine," Kendrick told him. "I've made up my mind that the enemy is much too foxy to do what we expect him to do. However, if you'll take over here, just as a precaution, I'd like to make another move up into the high country. There are two ends to that cattle trail, you know."

The round man's expression became anxious. "Do you still think Trappe is involved in this dirty business?"

"I don't know what to think. That's why I want to get as much information as I can—and immediately. Before we get any more moves from the enemy I'd like to know who they are."

"An admirable strategy," Mr. Glass approved. "We must, as it is so aptly put in *Henry the Fourth,* 'send discoverers forth to know the number of our enemies'."

Kendrick almost blew a mouthful of coffee back into the cup. "You and Mac!" he exclaimed. "So long. I'll see you after I've cleared the quotations out of my head in the high country."

This time he used the trail that had brought him down into the valley at the time of the raid. Once on the plateau he scouted carefully but the high country was peaceful, neither man nor beast showing. It took him less than twenty minutes to cut the trail which concerned him so much but when he saw it he knew that it should tell him something. A swift glance was enough. Three distinct sets of prints showed there, fresh sign made within the past day or so.

He dismounted to study the marks with some care. Two sets were those of a horseman headed toward the southern slope of the plateau while one was northbound. Comparison of the tracks suggested a round trip and he guessed that the paired marks were those of Amos Trappe's bronc. Maybe he hadn't actually seen Trappe on the secret trail but it sure looked as if the man had been using it!

The third set looked a little more recent but he had to follow the trace a good quarter of a mile before he found where the tracks overlay those which he believed to be Trappe's. So a rider had gone from NA's upper range down toward Packsaddle some hours after Amos Trappe made his trip. It suggested that Amos was being given the latest word on the man who had appeared at NA yesterday.

He moved with extra caution after that, realizing that he might meet the NA rider coming back. However nothing happened. The slope eased away to the south, the trail leading downhill on an easy angle and cutting westward toward the big bend of Packsaddle Creek. He couldn't see the town from that part of the mountain but he assumed that it must lie just beyond a shoulder of high ground.

Presently he eased into the flat land north of the creek's bend and recognized the territory. He had come down from the hill country only a short distance east of his own eastern boundary. The cattle trail wound through a thick stand of willows and crossed the creek, blending on the far side with another beaten path which he guessed must be the regular trail NA had been using under the terms of the original deal with Uncle Bill.

For a moment he wondered if he hadn't been dreaming up mysteries. NA cattle had simply been rounded up in two areas, the highlands and the creek bottoms. They had been driven by the trail which was most convenient, the two routes joining here along the creek. There was nothing wrong about it after all.

Then he noticed how the sign had been carefully blotted along the creek. Cattle from the high country had joined the regular trail at that point but they had forded the creek to make the junction. Anyone riding the regular trail would never notice that the junction was there. Not unless they crossed the creek to scout among the willows —and that didn't seem likely.

He went back to check more carefully on the sign left by Trappe and the other rider, discovering that both of them had played the same game. He could spot their sign into the willows but could find no trace of it on the far bank. On the main trail there were too many marks for him to be sure of anything but he knew no doubts. Both of them had used the hidden trail with caution, making certain that its connection with the creek trail was not disclosed by their movements. Now it had to mean something!

While he was pondering the situation he heard hoof-beats coming down the creek from the north and within a minute or two could see three riders approaching. His new partners were headed for Packsaddle again.

"Still got money to spend?" he greeted as they came close. "I thought you practically bought the town out yesterday."

"It's my notion," Jo told him soberly. "I simply can't settle down until I get some idea of the truth about Amos Trappe. If he was up on the mesa yesterday I want to know about it."

"So you're simply going to ride in and ask him?" Kendrick tried to keep the irony out of his voice.

"That's exactly what I propose to do," the girl told him, a tight set to her lips. "I find it difficult to believe that Amos is involved in anything as brutal as this seems to be and I don't want to go on being in doubt. I shall ask him directly and without beating around the bush."

Kendrick merely nodded, swinging his horse to fall in beside her as they went on toward Packsaddle. For the moment it didn't seem like a good idea to tell her about the things he had just seen. If she decided to believe what Trappe might tell her it would be better to have less cause for dispute between himself and her. Meanwhile he could do his own thinking.

Mr. Glass spoke from behind him. "Find anything up there on the mountain this morning?"

"Sagebrush and rocks," Kendrick replied over his shoulder. "Otherwise the place seemed deserted."

The reply seemed to satisfy both the girl and her father. Mac kept silent. Maybe that was one advantage of having an ex-gambler as a partner. A man who had learned to guard his tongue was a good sort to have around in a pinch like this one.

In spite of the early hour Packsaddle was astir when they rode in. Kendrick could scarcely believe his eyes. This bit of flat country south of the big hump had been

91

just another piece of creek bottom when he had seen it last. Now there was a town of perhaps thirty houses there. He noted two livery stables, three saloons, a couple of restaurants and several stores of various types in addition to the sprawling establishment which he realized was Amos Trappe's trading post and freight station. Clearly there had been a considerable boom during the past few years. Packsaddle was a real town and Amos Trappe's place was a fairly big enterprise.

"You want to talk to Amos alone?" Kendrick asked the girl.

She glanced toward him briefly, her expression a trifle tight. "No. I want this to be all out in the open."

It was a vain hope, he thought to himself. There were several people in this affair who didn't propose to let certain things come out into the open. Because he was one of them he felt uneasy about the role he was now playing. He did not comment, however, and the four riders pulled up in front of Trappe's main store, dismounting in a rather strained silence. Kendrick tried to throw off his own sense of guilt; it was no time to be having foolish scruples just when something might break. He wondered how Trappe was going to answer a question which was something of an indictment.

The trader met them just inside the door of a well stocked store. He was freshly shaven, neatly dressed and almost too polite. Kendrick tried to smother his quick resentment at sight of the man, realizing that perhaps he was being merely jealous. When a man is red-eyed and bewhiskered he doesn't enjoy the sight of an enemy looking spruce and dapper. Kendrick hoped that Amos Trappe was about to make a complete fool of himself.

Trappe bowed politely to the girl, pointedly ignoring the others. "Sorry I missed you yesterday, Jo," he greeted. "I was carrying out my promise."

"Your promise?" she repeated, frowning her question.

"Of course. I said I'd take steps to stop any troubles with NA. I did that very thing. Yesterday I rode across to their upper range by way of the mountain shoulder, trying to locate Floyd Mitchell. I figured I'd get matters squared away through him if I could let him know what we suspect. Mitchell happened to be down at the ranch house but I sent word to him by Dusty Gower. Dusty's an old hand with Floyd so I know he'll get things straight. Between them they'll root out the guilty parties; you can be sure there will be no more trouble from any NA men."

Kendrick smothered an impulse to swear. Trappe had put himself into the clear in an adroit maneuver. He had explained his moves in a way that sounded completely innocent, a way that Jo would probably accept at face value. Nor could Kendrick throw a reasonable doubt on the voluntary explanation. Trappe had not offered an excuse; he had simply stated his case. For the moment the burly trader held the advantage.

"We'll hope that your influence will be effective," Jo said after a brief pause. "Did you get any hint as to why they have been trying to hurt us?"

"I'm not even sure they did. I simply warned Mitchell that if any men on his payroll were guilty of those raids that he would have to find them and deal out punishment. There's always the chance that we were wrong in blaming NA riders, of course."

Kendrick expected the girl to take issue with him on that but she merely nodded. "Thank you. Did anyone tell you that Mr. Smith and Mr. Cavanagh have decided to throw in with us as partners on the homestead? We're going to have a real try at working the property."

That was a jolt for Trappe, Kendrick felt certain. The burly man frowned, not even trying to hide his displeasure. "Fool thing to do, Jo," he said. "You could've had capital if you'd asked for it. Bringing in strangers is no way to do business." His glare at Kendrick was a momentary thing but it told its story; Amos Trappe was jealous.

"Rather a partnership than a debt," Jo told him.

"Maybe you'd rather talk about it when Mac and I aren't here," Kendrick said dryly. "We'll take care of that other errand while you and Trappe talk." Nobody asked him what the other errand was and it was just as well; he didn't have one.

Smith followed him to the hitch rack and they mounted to ride down the rutted main street. Kendrick turned off at a lane which led toward the big freight sheds, making sure that no one was within hearing before he asked, "Is Amos jealous of the girl getting friendly with us or is he afraid we'll bust into some other game he's planning?"

Smith shrugged. "I'm no mind reader. You tell me."

"I think he's up to something a lot deeper than making a play for a pretty woman."

"What about his story just now? He had it real pat, didn't he?"

"Too pat. That's what burns me. I know he's lying. I know why he's lying. And at the moment I can't even say a word."

He explained about the trail he had followed earlier in the morning. "It's easy to figure. After Mitchell and Dusty were sure that I'd slipped through their ambush before they could set it they began to get suspicious that maybe I'd been up to a few other little errands. Maybe they spent the rest of the day working out my sign. They could figure real easy that I watched Trappe talking to Dusty. So one of them high-tails it down here to let Trappe know what they've found—and he gets himself a good yarn ready to tell. I'll bet he felt mighty smug when he saw us riding in this morning, giving him the perfect opportunity to spring his fairy tale when it would sound best!"

"The lady sure swallowed it."

"That's the worst of it! I figure he's been buying stolen stock from Floyd Mitchell, likely working it in with legitimate beef. The hidden trail would be perfect for such a job. But how would anybody prove it on him?"

"Think your uncle tumbled to what was going on?"

"Probably. That's why they murdered him." Kendrick's jaw was tight as he growled the words. Thinking about Uncle Bill only made it harder to swallow the fact that Amos Trappe was clearing himself so cleverly.

"I think there's more," Smith said quietly.

"Sure. They've pulled a complete switch now, trying to make it look as though some outside outfit had been pulling all of the dirty work."

"More than that, I mean. Take a look at the Trappe place. It's big, too big for the kind of business he seems to be doing. The profits out of this trading post don't let

94

him swagger around the way he does—and a two-bit rustling game can't be the answer either. What's the rest of it?"

Kendrick came to a quick decision. "Tell Jo that I've gone scouting," he said shortly. "Look for me back in a couple of days. I'm going to make a visit to Cimarron. Maybe I'll pick up a hint there."

12

THE little man nodded his understanding but continued to ride beside Kendrick as they passed the length of Trappe's warehouses. Most of the area was deserted this morning but they could see into several of the sheds. Kendrick commented once. "Steam sawmill in there," he said, pointing to some uncrated bits of machinery. "Looks like Amos figures the boom is going to last."

"Seems so," Smith agreed. "I was in one of the back rooms of the store yesterday and I noticed a lot of axes and hand saws. Must be the building business figures to grow a lot."

"We'll keep it in mind," Kendrick nodded. "My Spanish strip has some of the best timber in this country. It could be that the piece of land our murderous friends want is the ridge rather than the valley. See if you can get some kind of a line on these building plans."

Smith nodded and pulled up, watching Kendrick ride on out of town toward the lower angle of Spanish Ridge. There was a branch of the creek which wound around south of the ridge proper but Kendrick was going to take the short cut over the ridge, partly because it would save him a little time and partly because he wanted to reassure himself on that timber matter. His impression was that the ridge had some pretty big stuff on it, the kind of timber which might be valuable if anyone wanted to saw out beams and other heavy timbers.

He left the well marked trail which he knew led to the

new gold camps on Van Bremer's Creek, the depth of the ruts attesting to the volume of traffic which had been building up Amos Trappe's business. It was pretty clear that Trappe had planned smartly when he moved his trading post from the old Santa Fe Trail up into this edge of the mountains. Here he had a monopoly on the supply trade to the mining valleys and he was in position to control trade to either homestead or cattle developments. When the railroad pushed south over Raton Pass there would be an even greater opportunity for a man well established on a good feeder line.

Suddenly Kendrick realized what he had been missing in the picture. That approaching railroad was a factor he hadn't been considering. The Santa Fe would need a lot of timber when they started running their rail south toward Las Vegas. Cross ties, bridge timbers, supports for water towers—they would be in the market for plenty! And there was no big stuff anywhere along the route to the east. For that matter, there was not too much anywhere. The stands of pinion offered nothing to the construction man. Most of the yellow pine and spruce pine was too small for heavy timbers. Kendrick knew of no decent quantity of big lumber anywhere in this part of the territory except the stuff on Spanish Ridge.

He did some mental arithmetic as he let his horse work slowly up the first slopes of the rise. Figuring one cross tie every two feet made twenty-six hundred and forty ties to the mile. From Raton Pass to Wagon Mound was about sixty miles. For that stretch alone the construction crews would need more than a hundred and fifty thousand ties, not allowing for spurs or branch lines of any kind. Even allowing for some faults in his hasty arithmetic it was clear that the Santa Fe Railroad people were going to be in the market for a staggering quantity of ties. With few trees in the region big enough to rip out a railroad tie it became certain that the timber on Spanish Ridge was going to be valuable. No wonder Amos Trappe had imported a sawmill and lumbering tools—no wonder somebody wanted to get control of the ridge!

Kendrick had half a mind to cut back and pass the word of his idea to his partners but decided against it.

There would be plenty of time for talk later. Other moves were indicated.

He swung hard up the slope as he reached the ridge proper, entering a good stand of spruce pine within a matter of five minutes. Everywhere the trees were thick, tall and straight. Perfect for timbers and capable of making any quantity of good ties. He followed the crest of the ridge for something more than a mile, satisfying himself that there was really plenty of the big stuff up there. Then he swung to the west once more and headed for Cimarron.

By that time his mind was active with other questions. If Amos Trappe had his eye on the ridge was he also an active party in the campaign to get rid of the ridge's owner? Was there a double connection between the rustling of NA beef and the man who had almost certainly been buying it on the quiet? Who had really been responsible for the deaths of Uncle Bill and Ed Cavanagh—the NA riders or Amos Trappe?

It reminded him of another point which he had been neglecting in the confusion of events and ideas. Ed Cavanagh had known that his masquerade was due for an unmasking. He might have told Trappe about that letter from Kendrick. Trappe's game would be quite different if he knew that Kendrick was still alive.

After thinking it over for a couple of miles Kendrick came to the conclusion that Cavanagh had kept his jolt to himself. Probably he had planned to get away with whatever he could salvage from his unfortunate attempt at fraud and it seemed likely that he would have kept his plans completely secret. So Trappe didn't know. He wouldn't suspect that the real owner of the ridge was alive. Maybe that was why he was paying such ardent court to Jo. Marrying the owner-of-record would be a pretty good way of getting hold of the ridge.

Kendrick made an early camp that evening, his ribs sore from so much riding. By the time he stretched out beside a fire, easing himself comfortably on thick pine needles, he knew that he'd been right on one item at least. Since leaving Spanish Ridge he hadn't seen more than a dozen pines large enough for respectable construction timbers and not more than a hundred big enough for good ties. Spanish Ridge was the key.

On the deeper implications he couldn't be so certain. He guessed that Trappe had been involved with the NA cattle thieves and had used his connections there for his own purposes, perhaps convincing Mitchell and the others that they should try to scare off the owner of the homestead which was so close to their rustling trail. With that point in mind it was possible to guess at any number of circumstances which might have led to the two deaths. Kendrick inclined toward the belief that Cavanagh hadn't known of the crooked deal. He'd simply been a victim of a plot that was much deeper than he had believed it to be.

It was mid-afternoon of the following day when Kendrick reached Cimarron, taking time for a quick meal at an adobe restaurant before making his way to the territorial land office. To his satisfaction he recognized the official in charge as being the same man he had dealt with some six years earlier. It seemed too much to hope that the man would have an equally good memory but Kendrick decided to play for that point.

"I came to see you about a piece of property on Packsaddle Creek, Senor Ramirez," he announced after a quiet greeting. "Maybe you'll remember me. My name is Thomas Kendrick. I was here in 'seventy-one."

The New Mexican stared at Kendrick. He was a tall, olive-skinned man of perhaps fifty, one of those philosophical persons who accepted changes of fortune without much murmur but with an eye to his own legitimate advantage. Kendrick knew that he had used his education and his excellent command of the English language to full value since the Americans had been coming into the territory in large numbers. He was also reputed to be an honest official.

"I seem to recall you quite well," Ramirez said, frowning perplexedly. "I also remember the name. If you are Kendrick, how does it happen that I recall the recent report of your death?"

"That's easy," Kendrick told him. "I was reported dead. Twice, as a matter of fact. The first time I was wrongly believed to be dead. The second time a dead

98

man was wrongly believed to be me. So far I'm still alive."

"And you really are Thomas Kendrick? Please, I do not wish to doubt your word but it is many years since I saw you. I am sure that you are not the man who came here as Thomas Kendrick less than a year ago."

"Then you met the fellow who appeared as claimant to the Hockett property?"

Senor Ramirez was still staring, obviously trying to untangle his own confused memory. "I met him. At the time I seemed to remember my first meeting with you and I felt . . . However, the time was far back and this man was well identified."

"By Amos Trappe?"

"Exactly. If I have failed in my duty I did so because I was badly deceived."

"It was no fault of yours," Kendrick soothed, elated that he should have found the official so easily convinced. Proof of his identity could have been produced easily enough but this way was simpler. He decided to take Ramirez completely into his confidence. He made no reference in his story to the trouble at the homestead but he was explicit about the Cavanagh masquerade.

Ramirez was slightly aghast at the news. "I have issued a deed to an imposter," he murmured worriedly. "But the man looked like the one I thought I remembered. He was much like you, I am sure. And he had the Senor Trappe to vouch for him."

"Like I said," Kendrick told him with a crooked smile, "you've got nothing to worry about. After all, what did you do except to certify that a piece of property formerly owned by William Hockett should now vest in one Thomas Kendrick according to the will of said Hockett? I'm that Thomas Kendrick. I thank you for taking care of my interests through my agent who appeared before you last summer."

Ramirez squinted thoughtfully and then laughed aloud. "It is as you say. The man who pretended to be you simply rushed the processes of the law. The property is in your name." Then his frown came back again. "But what of the widow of whom I have heard? It is understood that this other Kendrick married and that his widow is to claim his property."

"It's a point to be considered," Kendrick told him gravely. "I am not dead. So my widow can't claim my property. That is logical, I think."

Again Ramirez nodded, his smile breaking through again. "It is logical but for me it is not enough. I am but the clerk. I keep the records. If this woman comes to me and demands this property what am I to do?"

"Just tell her she is not a widow. At least she's not the widow she thinks she is. Ask her for proof of the death of Thomas Kendrick."

"But this other man? Do you not wish . . . ?"

"Let's play it the cautious way, senor. Pretend you don't know about what we have discussed here today. Simply demand proof of the title holder's death. If she happens to have some kind of statement from someone around Packsaddle you can refuse to accept it as not being sufficiently formal. All we want is a little delay."

"But . . . "

"It's best this way, believe me. You can get in touch with the army authorities if you still have your doubts about me. It will be no trouble to prove that the man who called himself Kendrick was here at a time when the army had Kendrick listed as dead. Other records will show that Kendrick was at Fort Russell and Cheyenne when this other man was living here under the name of Kendrick."

"I believe you, senor. I simply want to keep my records properly. It is my job, you know."

"Sure. You can't afford to get them messed up with false claims—like the one you filed on the strength of Amos Trappe's statement. Better go along with me and hope that I can untangle the whole business before you have to get mixed up any worse."

He had to do a bit of arguing but eventually the New Mexican agreed to carry out Kendrick's plan. Actually Kendrick wondered why he should be trying so hard to get his scheme accepted. He hadn't the least idea what good it was going to do.

There was a good three hours of daylight left to him

100

after he finished his interview with the registrar of deeds so he hit the trail at once, planning to swing back into the hills on the way east in an effort to make sure about his assumptions regarding the timber situation. With a three-hour start on the morrow's ride he could make the detour and still reach Packsaddle Creek in one day.

It worried him a little that he was leaving the homestead partly unguarded for so long but it seemed like a good time to take the risk. Trappe would feel fairly safe after having played his hand so cleverly—and anyway the NA gang were now principally interested in getting the man who had spied on them. Probably they would make no new attack until they could hit the main object of their concern.

He swung a little to the north, threading canyons where prospect holes showed bare among the trees or where prospectors still worked, hopeful of finding some of the gold or silver that had turned up only a little distance to the northwest. Kendrick was interested to see this show of industry in the land but he was more concerned with the obvious fact that the timber seemed small. Spanish Ridge was still the key point.

A full day of riding gave him no reason to change his mind on any major point although he did become a little restless as he neared his objective. Too much delay was something to be avoided. With the Santa Fe people already grading Raton Pass it seemed likely that they would be sending their advance men into the area before long, searching out the construction supplies they would need for the drive south. Trappe would be anticipating such a move and would be anxious to get title to the strategic bit of timber.

The afternoon shadows were lengthening when he found himself at last on Spanish Ridge. Having come in from an unfamiliar angle, he did not know his exact position but as he started down the eastern slope he caught a glimpse of the valley and knew that he was a mile or so above the homestead claims. Because the valley trail would be easier to follow in the growing dusk he took the direct downgrade, letting his tired horse coast along to suit himself.

101

He was almost down to the valley when his ear caught a significant combination of sounds just below him. A man had yelled a hoarse command and a steer had bawled in protest. He pulled up sharply, listening to what he knew were the noises of a trail herd being moved along the creek. The sounds were coming closer; the herd was being shoved down the valley.

He dismounted and led his horse, cutting across at a slight angle so as to intercept the drive a little more to the south. When the sounds told him that he was close to the movement but still above it he kept pace, waiting for a break in the trees. When he found it he pulled up, watching as the drive moved past. Three riders were handling only fourteen head of stock, easing them along quietly and with no sign of haste even though night was coming on.

The hint was too broad to be ignored. This was no regular drive. Kendrick moved down behind them, keeping his interval but at the same time staying far enough up the slope to have good cover among the trees. It was awkward travel now with the gloom thickening but there was no need for haste. The trail herd was moving slowly and in about a quarter mile stopped entirely.

Kendrick tied his horse to a tree and went forward on foot, listening to the cautious shouts of the riders. He feared that he had made his move too late to hear the important talk between them but he did manage to catch the final orders to the one man who was apparently slated to stay with the cattle.

"You'll know when to bust 'em loose," a familiar rasping voice growled. "Run 'em down a bit to make sure they head in the right direction. Then pick up the ropes and come to meet us. Could be we'll need every man; that polecat's a tough one."

"I'll be ready," another voice agreed. "But don't be too long about it. I got no hankerin' to play nursemaid fer them critters half the night."

"Keep yer shirt on! We got to find out a few things before we make any moves. And it could be a lot healthier if we let 'em settle down before we start things to poppin'. You tend to yer cows and stay awake!"

The speaker and another rider swung away to ride back up the trail, passing within a few yards of the spot where Kendrick lay hidden. That harsh angry voice had been too familiar for doubt. Floyd Mitchell and his NA renegades were up to some new trick. Judging by the few words he had overheard, it was shaping up to be just as deadly as the earlier ones.

13

FOR a few minutes Kendrick practically held his breath, fearful that his picketed horse might make some sound that would betray his position to the backtracking pair. When the moment of danger passed he relaxed a little and began to move in on the cattle. There was still enough light for him to see the guard adjusting the lariats which formed a hasty corral for the animals.

It was no trick to move close to the NA man's horse and when the fellow came back from his rope job he suddenly found a six-gun aimed at his middle. "Get your hands way up!" Kendrick snapped. "And turn around! Fast!"

The astonished man obeyed orders. In the darkness Kendrick could not be sure but he had a feeling that this was the fellow he had seen wearing the bright blue shirt, the one they had called Dusty.

"Now hold it right there," he went on. "No wrong moves unless you want a slug in your back."

He moved in quickly, pulling the other man's gun and transferring it to his own belt. "Now," he said, "want to talk a little bit? Maybe you could save yourself some of the grief that's coming to your crooked pards if you spoke a real nice piece at this point."

"Who're you?" the man growled. "What's goin' on here?"

"I'm Tom Kendrick. The other question is for you to answer."

"Kendrick? That's crazy! Kendrick's dead. Floyd . . . "

He broke off abruptly but Kendrick had heard enough. "Wrong, my stupid friend. The man Floyd Mitchell killed was pretending to be Kendrick. If your friend Amos Trappe had been playing fair with you he'd have told you the truth. Amos knew."

"In that case," the other man muttered, "I might as well . . . "

He was whirling as he spoke, evidently hopeful of catching Kendrick off guard with his pretense of surrender. One wild swing glanced off the side of Kendrick's head but then the surprise was over and Kendrick used the gun as a club, knocking his man sprawling with it.

"Lucky for you I didn't want to do any shooting," he grumbled, stooping down to poke carefully at his fallen opponent. The man lay still but Kendrick took no further chances, rolling him over and pinning his hands behind him while he tied him up with his own bandanna. As a further precaution he hoisted him to the back of the waiting horse and lashed him fast, using a rope which apparently had not been needed for the improvised cattle pen.

Then Kendrick stumbled back through the darkness to his own mount. He wasn't exactly sure what he ought to do with the prisoner but it seemed like a good idea to take him along. With a little persuasion of the right kind he might talk.

Locating his horse was a matter of a few moments and presently he was in the saddle again, leading the other bronc with its inert load. Now he had to move a bit faster. Some kind of attack was in preparation and he had to warn the folks at the homestead cabins.

There was no light in either place when he broke out into the open and for a moment he was tempted to duck back into cover for a bit of preliminary scouting. Maybe the raiders had already shown themselves. Then he changed his mind. There was no time for delaying tactics; he had to pass the word.

He was within a hundred yards of his own place when he heard a movement in the darkness ahead. Drawing his six-gun he crouched a little lower, staring into the gloom. Someone had moved at the corner of the corral.

"Is that you, Mac?" he called, ready to blast away if the words brought a shot in reply.

It was a relief to hear the little man's quick laugh. "Right enough. Advance, and be recognized."

"We're due for some company," Kendrick called softly.

Smith emerged from his shadow, staring at the led horse. "Looks like we've got company already. Who's your friend and is he dead?"

"I think it's a lad named Dusty Gower and he's alive. I'm counting on him for some talk when he gets over his headache." He swung down from the saddle, explaining matters as he stripped the gear from his horse and led it into the corral.

"I figure they're planning to dust us off good this time. They've got some NA beef just above the valley and they'll turn it loose so that it'll be found here after the fight. Then they can claim we stole it and they shot us up in trying to recover the rustled stock. At least that's the way it looks to me right now."

"The idea being that we won't be alive to contradict the story," Mac added quietly. "Sounds like a real cozy scheme. When do we expect them?"

"That part I didn't hear. Maybe we can pry it out of Dusty. Where's the rest of the partnership?"

"Cimarron, I reckon. They left for there at daybreak this morning."

"I didn't think she was in any hurry to get that matter fixed up," Kendrick said, a little surprised.

"Trappe sold her a bill of goods, I imagine," Smith told him dryly. "They must have had quite a confab after we left them in the store together and the lady seemed to think Amos had squared himself completely. She simply said she wanted to get the title fixed up and I didn't argue the point. There wasn't any call for me to say anything anyway."

Kendrick wondered briefly how Ramirez would handle the business but at the moment there were more vital matters than the legal proceedings at Cimarron.

"Let's get our friend into the cabin," he said. "I think this is beginning to shape up a bit."

They put the NA bronc into the corral and carried the unconscious Dusty into the little cabin. The man was beginning to breathe noisily so Kendrick doused him with some cold water and waited for him to stir. He had to judge by the sounds because he didn't want to strike a light.

Presently the prisoner started to mutter and Kendrick prodded him with his toe. "Ready to talk, Gower?" he asked, hoping to get a reaction by using the name.

"Who's that?"

"Kendrick. Same one who cracked you on the head a while ago. Want to tell us a few things or do you want to get slugged again?"

"I got nothin' to say." The man, apparently fully conscious now, sounded sullen.

"Better change your mind," Kendrick advised. "You're in the cabin with us now. When your boys start shooting you'll be right in the line of fire. We'll make sure of that."

"Don't seem as how we need any talk from him," Smith said quietly. "We got a good line on what Mitchell wants. We know how he works. They'll try to gun you down; we set up to block the deal. It's simple as that."

"Not quite," Kendrick replied, talking partly for the benefit of the man on the floor. "I figure this is another one of those jobs where Amos Trappe is using Mitchell for a sucker. Since I saw you last I figured out what Trappe's game really is. He wants the timberland on Spanish Ridge. Instead of making his own move to get it he uses the rustling connection so as to have Mitchell do his dirty work for him."

"You mean Trappe planned this latest move?"

"I'd bet on it. Trappe passed the word to Mitchell that now's a good time to raid the place while the girl and her father are out of the way. Trappe would like to see both buildings burned—and both of us killed. That would leave the girl without much chance of hanging on here."

"Then he still doesn't know who you are?"

"Likely not. Although it could work the other way. Maybe he wants to get rid of me before I can declare myself. Then he could still make a deal with Jo. Either way, he puts it up to Mitchell to get rid of the man who can talk too much. Mitchell is willing enough, seeing as how I threaten to queer his crooked game at NA."

"Sounds like you got it figured out. You think Mitchell knows that you picked up his little playmate here?"

"No. Dusty's our ace-in-the-hole. He'll make good bullet bait when the fight starts."

The man on the floor spoke suddenly. "Maybe we could make a deal."

"What deal?" Kendrick didn't sound very receptive to the proposition.

"Let me get a head start outa this damn country and I'll tell you Floyd's plan."

"Why should we believe you?"

"No reason." He was being ruefully honest about it. "I just heard enough so I can put two and two together. I reckon some of us have been gettin' played fer suckers and I'm declarin' myself out."

Smith laughed. "Declaring yourself out and getting out are two different things, friend! You're in—up to the neck that's apt to get stretched."

"I'm serious," the man insisted. "I admit I was in on the plan to steal NA beef. Nobody worries much about snakin' out a few head of stock that belongs to a bunch of foreign millionaires. I didn't figure to get tangled up in no killin's, though."

"Go ahead," Kendrick invited. "Let's hear the story."

"First you got to promise to let me go."

"Like fun we do!" Smith snapped. "I think we'll just tie you up and fix it so you can't let out a peep. Then we'll lock you up in the other cabin while we hole up in this one. If your gang sets fire to the other place you'll start frying even before you reach the place where it looks like you'll be going." He nudged Kendrick in the darkness as he made the threat.

"I'll talk," Dusty promised earnestly. "You got it straight on tonight's raid. The plan is to burn out both cabins and make sure that neither of you jaspers are around to talk when it's over. I was supposed to turn the NA stock loose in the valley after dark so it'd look like you got caught rustlin'. That'd square Mitchell with the boss."

"Just like I guessed it," Kendrick told him. "Now let's have the rest of the story and maybe we won't let you burn until your natural time comes."

Gower seemed to have surrendered completely. He told his story with no attempt to keep himself out of it but with frequent references to Floyd Mitchell as the brains of the rustling outfit. Evidently he had not thought of Amos Trappe as anyone except the receiver of the rustled beef.

At first the game had been simple. The NA renegades would drive the stolen stock down to Packsaddle by way of the hidden trail and Trappe would cover up easily enough, mixing stolen stock with NA beef he had bought. Then Hockett had seen the rustlers coming down across the meadow to the creek with a bunch of cattle. Mitchell had promptly ordered the raid in which Hockett had been shot down. Dusty and the other NA men hadn't expected the killing. They had thought the game was to scare Hockett into keeping quiet and at the same time make it appear that some sort of organized rustling gang was operating against both NA and the homesteader. With Hockett dead they had to keep quiet or be subject to punishment as accessories.

Then Ed Cavanagh had entered the picture under the name of Kendrick. Trappe had assured the NA crew that the newcomer would offer no problem to them. It was generally understood that Trappe had the new man under his thumb but in late winter the orders were changed. The man known as Kendrick had to go. A cattle-killing raid was not a sufficiently strong hint so a second attack was made, the result similar to the Hockett affair. By that time the NA riders were in so deep they couldn't argue with the orders they were getting. Dusty insisted that he had not suspected Trappe's real interest in the matter but had taken his orders from Mitchell only.

"Now will you let me get out of here?" he whined. "I've told you all I know. Gimme a couple of hours' start, that's all I ask."

"Don't get hasty," Smith told him. "We want to know

a lot of things before we lose the pleasure of your company."

"If we lose it," Kendrick added. "Maybe it would be better to have him around for the showdown."

"Then I ain't goin' to tell you nothin'!" The prisoner suddenly became defiant. "I'll talk if you'll promise to let me get away but I won't spill another word unless I'm goin' to get clear."

There was a rustle in the darkness, a squeak of leather as Smith knelt over the prisoner. Kendrick opened his mouth to ask a question but suddenly Dusty let out a yell of pain. Smith's voice came calmly, reproachfully. "Now, now! 'This ague-fit of fear is overblown.' That's from *Macbeth*. But you're not hurt—at least not like you're going to be unless you open up."

"But I got to get away from here or none of this is goin' to do me any good."

"You sound fearful, my friend. 'Death we fear. That makes these odds all even.' Or if you don't like *Measure for Measure* I'll give you another one from *Macbeth*: 'Our fears do make us traitors.' So talk fast before I start putting some more fear of death into your yellow heart!"

Kendrick wanted to chuckle, particularly because Smith had come around to place a warning hand on his arm. The little man was having himself quite a time talking tough and quoting Shakespeare at the same time. However, the prisoner's yell of pain had hinted that the threat was not an empty one.

"What d'you want to know that I didn't tell you?" Dusty demanded.

"When do your thugs attack? How many of them will be in the gang? How much does Craddock really know about this business?"

Kendrick suddenly cut in to ask, "Which one of you hustled down to Packsaddle to let Trappe know I'd seen him up among the crags?"

Dusty surrendered again, answering the questions sullenly but with details which made them sound reasonably credible. The assault on the two cabins was due to begin at midnight. There would be five men in addition to Mitchell. Two of them were to set fire to the Hockett

109

cabin while the other four were to wait outside the Kendrick place, ready to shoot down the men who might be expected to rush out when the fire started. The rustler outfit numbered eight altogether but Dave Neal—with his wounded arm—would be passing the alarm to Craddock, notifying him that NA cattle had been stolen by the people down the creek. Dusty himself would be out of the fight because he had the job of shoving the NA beef into the valley where they would be discovered by Craddock when he arrived on the scene.

They hammered questions at the prisoner, trying to trip him up on some part of the story but nothing shook him. He handed out extra information on the subject of the way Trappe had recently seemed to dictate the movements of the band but there was nothing in his statements that Kendrick had not already guessed. At the moment none of those facts was important; the immediate concern was the defense of the two cabins.

"We'll work it this way," Kendrick said after a time. "One of us will go over to Uncle Bill's place and hole up there. The other one stays here—and doesn't go out under any circumstances. The man here will have more of a war party after his scalp but he ought to get some help from the other cabin. That big rifle of Uncle Bill's can toss a slug this far. If our busy friends start throwing fire around we'll have light to shoot by and maybe we can make 'em a bit unhappy. Which job do you want?"

"I'll take this one."

"You've got four men to meet instead of two."

"What about me?" Dusty called from the spot in the corner where Smith had rolled him. "When do I git away?"

"After we find out if you've told us the truth," Mac retorted. "Stop fussing or I'll quote some more Shakespeare at you!"

"He's your prisoner," Kendrick said shortly. "Turn him loose when it's safe—and if he didn't lie to us. I'll be getting over to the other place while we've still got time to get ready."

14

A FEW stars shone dimly in the eastern sky but the west was completely overcast when Kendrick started across toward the Hockett cabin, leading his horse and listening for sounds that might indicate the presence of the enemy. Maybe the attack was not to take place until midnight but he didn't think it was a good idea to bank too heavily on Dusty's word.

But there was no sign of trouble around and he led his horse into the other corral without incident. The two work horses were there but no other saddle horses, Jo and her father having taken their mounts for the trip to Cimarron.

He made his preparations carefully, barricading every window and door of the cabin except the back one. Then he went outside to sit in the darkness with the Navy Springfield across his knees.

It was only a little after ten when he took up his position by the rain barrel at the corner of the cabin, wondering idly why the barrel was still there. Since the installation of the pump there had been little use for the older water supply—even when there was rain enough to maintain it.

He tried to keep his thoughts from wandering to such meaningless matters, concentrating on the problem at hand. They should be able to beat off Mitchell's attack, the element of surprise being with the defense. It still wouldn't settle everything. Trappe was practically in the clear on the whole deal.

The trader had played his hand shrewdly, using the rustler gang as a cover for his own schemes at the same time that he took a profit from their activities. Indeed, Trappe had been smart all the way, playing Cavanagh's game in the same way that he had played up to Mitchell —with the ultimate profits of Amos Trappe always in mind. He had even turned that last bit of evidence against him to a point in his favor, somehow using it to persuade Jo that she must push that matter of taking title to the land.

Then a sober thought struck home. In his concern over learning Floyd Mitchell's attack plans he hadn't considered the role which Trappe might play in this night's work. And certainly Trappe would declare himself in. The man was playing for big stakes, the control or ownership of the Spanish strip with its big timber. His connections with the NA rustlers were possible embarrassments. He couldn't hope to make any further small profits by the purchase of their stolen beef—but a disclosure of the rustler operation might ruin him completely. If Trappe was so vitally interested in getting the rustling game saved from possible exposure was it likely that he would trust the whole thing to Mitchell?

The answer was obvious but it also suggested another question. Would Trappe trust Mitchell—or anyone else—to keep quiet after the immediate danger was over?

Why hadn't he thought of that sooner, Kendrick wondered. Maybe he could have made some use of the idea. . . .

A quick spatter of rain struck the backs of his hands and he looked up quickly, getting the drizzle in his face. The valley was darker now. He couldn't make out the silhouettes of either highland. Maybe that was a bit of good luck; the enemy would have to attack under adverse conditions.

It might make another difference, he realized. With rain coming on they might make the attack sooner, figuring that their fires would have to be set before the cabins could get wet. He wished he could pass the warning on to Smith but he didn't want to leave his post now. Mac would have to get along as best he could.

A half hour passed and then he heard a thin clink of metal as a shod hoof struck a bit of rock. The enemy was moving in.

He was getting pretty well dampened by that time but it did not bother him. Spare cartridges were well covered. What troubled him more than anything else was his grow-

112

ing conviction that Amos Trappe was planning to take a hand in tonight's action. It wouldn't be enough just to fight off Mitchell's gun hands; he had to be ready for extra trouble from Trappe.

Then he heard a voice. The rustlers, not expecting to find anyone around the Hockett place, weren't making any effort at stealth. "Get the stuff along the wall pronto," someone ordered. "If it gets any wetter we won't be able to light it."

In the blackness he could distinguish three horses and for a moment he thought Dusty had lied about the division of attacking forces. Then he realized that two of the horses carried riders while the third was a pack animal bearing a load of brush.

He could have picked off either man without trouble but he couldn't bring himself to do it. He waited until they were within twenty feet, both men dismounting and turning to unload the pack horse. Then he blasted away with his six-gun, fanning it empty while the rifle still lay across his lap.

The result was satisfying. He had aimed at the knees— or at least he had pointed in that general direction, knowing that real aim while fanning a gun was quite impossible. Both men went down, cursing in pain and alarm. All three horses bolted. A single shot came from one of the men on the ground, the slug hammering into the logs well above Kendrick's head.

"Where's he at?" a voice gasped. "Git him! I got a busted laig."

The gun slammed again and this time Kendrick replied, using the rifle to aim at the orange flash. A violent threshing and some extra cursing told him he had done damage so he slipped around the other side of the rain barrel, calling out, "Better give up. You're dead ducks if you try to fight it out."

There was no reply except for the muttered curses so he ordered, "Crawl toward the house. Leave your guns behind you."

"I can't move," a voice groaned. "Got a busted laig, I tell you!"

"Crawl!" Kendrick ordered harshly, aware that riders

113

were moving across the valley toward the scene. He had broken up the plan of attack but now it seemed certain that he would have to stand off the whole gang. Probably they were figuring that the other cabin had been left untenanted tonight. "One of you light a match and show me you're not bringing guns! Hustle it up or I'll start throwing lead again!"

He could hear a whispered argument going on but the man who seemed to be groaning more loudly was also the more determined. He struck a match in spite of a sharp order from his companion and Kendrick had a split second in which to see the other fellow's move. Two shots came from the belligerent one, the first cutting down the match holder while the second one slammed into the logs beside Kendrick. This time Kendrick had a good target and no mercy. The Springfield boomed again and then the night was still. Still, that is, except for those drumming hoofbeats that were now so close.

"What the devil's goin' on over here?" a harsh voice yelled. "Mike! Freck! Where are you?"

It was Mitchell; Kendrick could see him as a blur in the night. He slid back around the corner of the cabin, reloading his six-gun and jamming it into his belt before dropping a fresh shell into the breach of the Springfield. Then he shouted, "You're too late, Mitchell. Trappe warned us you'd be coming." He sighted around the corner and sent one of the fifty-caliber slugs toward the NA man.

The hoofbeats changed tempo as Mitchell retreated and again there was a brief moment of silence. This time a pair of shots from the other cabin ended the lull. Somewhere on that side of the valley a man shouted but at the distance Kendrick couldn't tell what the yell meant. Somehow it sounded unhappy so he guessed that Mac had opened his defensive operations in good style.

The minutes dragged by slowly and Kendrick circled the house with due caution, trying to make sure that he was not surprised from any angle. Then he moved across toward the corral, stopping on the way to check on the pair who had come to fire the cabin. Both were dead. That left four active raiders in the valley, he figured.

The quartet ought to be somewhat confused by this time. They had met opposition at both cabins and the taunt about Amos Trappe should have had some effect. They wouldn't know what their next move ought to be— but they would have to make one. According to their plans, Craddock would be getting his summons within a few minutes. They couldn't afford to have him arrive and find a battle still in progress. The whole scheme depended on the lack of any witnesses for the defense.

"Likely I'll get it," Kendrick told himself. "Most of the shooting has been here so they'll figure this is the spot they've got to clean out first."

He could hear riders moving at several places now. They had ceased any effort at further concealment and he tried to guess from the movements what they were planning to do. One man was probably going to find out what had happened to Dusty Gower but the other sounds were not so easy to interpret.

The activity lasted for perhaps twenty minutes and then there was a brisk exchange of fire from the other cabin. Again he had to make his guess from the subsequent shouting. Mac still seemed to be holding out.

Then he noticed a difference in the noises of the night. Two riders had halted somewhere just to the north of the corral and a third one had circled off to the east. That should have accounted for all but one of the remaining raiders but he was sure that the hoofbeats down the creek were the sounds of several horses. Maybe Amos Trappe was getting ready to take a hand. How strong a force he could throw into the fight was a matter still to be determined. Probably he had plenty of men ready for just such an affair.

Suddenly the pattern of movement erupted into more gunfire, this time to the south. At least three guns took part in the exchange, seven or eight shots being fired before a dead silence fell upon the valley.

One of the riders who had halted north of the corral promptly rode off in the direction of the shooting and again Kendrick waited and listened, trying to estimate the position of the enemy as well as the next move. Once he heard the sound of a vague movement in the general

115

direction of the other cabin but otherwise nothing was happening.

He was content to let it go that way. Time was working for him. If Mitchell and his gang did not make a general assault before long it would be too late. Daylight and the coming of Craddock would put the whole deadly scheme out of timing.

An hour passed and the rain began to slacken until he was not even sure that it was still raining. Being already wet made it difficult to judge. At least the danger of any quick fire was lessened.

Then he began to hear those furtive sounds of movement again. Now it was harder to be sure about them because a light breeze had begun to stir across the valley and the sounds were not so easily located.

He calculated that the hour was between two and three when the big push started. Two quick shots from the direction of the other cabin signaled the assault and instantly Kendrick could hear the thunder of hoofs as men drove in on him from three sides. He guessed they would be aiming at the cabin so he held his position at the corral, hopeful of knocking down at least one enemy before they could spot him.

They almost fooled him, two of them coming directly to the corral as though intending to use it as a vantage point for their attacking fire. He knocked one out of the saddle with his rifle but then had to fight a running pistol battle with the man who drove in from the opposite side. Twice he felt the jerk of bullets in the slack of his shirt but there was no accompanying pain. He aimed a careful shot at a dark form. The man went sprawling and Kendrick turned to meet another rider who had come thundering around from the far side of the cabin.

He shouldered against a corral post, trying to reload in the darkness while desperate fingers insisted on doing wrong things with the cartridges. Fortunately the new enemy could not spot him in the gloom, wasting a shot at the loose horse of one of the other raiders. Then a wounded man called a warning and the horseman swung toward the corral, orange flashes splitting the night as he came.

Kendrick held grimly on the dark shadow, not sure how many shells he actually had in his revolver. A splinter from a corral post cut his neck before he let the first shot go, wasting it as he flinched. Then he drew fine and fired again, cutting his man out of the saddle as he whirled past. One of the others fired from his position on the ground and Kendrick ran for the shelter of the house.

Firing continued from the other side of the valley so he judged that Smith was still taking good care of himself. For the moment he seemed to have no active enemies left so he halted to reload both weapons. There was no way of knowing how many fresh men Trappe had brought into the valley so he had to be ready for anything.

There was bitter satisfaction in the thought that at last both lots of crooks had been driven into the open. If the defense could hold out for another few hours there might be an end to the whole miserable business.

Then the distant firing subsided and he began to wonder about the guesses he had been making. Some of that shooting had not been near the cabin. Maybe Trappe's men had blundered against the rustlers and the two gangs had shot at each other. Maybe things were better than they seemed.

He contented himself with more watching and waiting, his eyes and ears alert to anything that might indicate a new move on the part of either enemy group. The first alarm came from close at hand and he heard movements near the corral which told him that his recent foes were trying to get away. He could hear enough of their talk to let him know that two wounded men were helping each other, trying to reach a horse which had not stampeded completely out of reach. The third man was dead and they were leaving him behind.

He heard them when they caught the horse and managed to climb to the animal's back. Then the retreat was easy to trace until the hoofbeats died away in the steady patter of falling rain.

Ten minutes later a gun slammed three times in quick succession, a hoarse yell being blotted out by the final shot. Kendrick guessed that the retreating wounded men

117

had run into a quick-triggered fellow crook and had been cut down without warning. He didn't know whether to be glad or sorry.

He moved to the back door of the cabin then, trying to get a bit of shelter from the continuing drizzle. When no sound came to warn of further attacks he risked a trip into the house, fumbling in a familiar closet for dry clothes. At first all his chilled fingers could encounter were women's garments but then he found a shirt that seemed familiar. Probably an old army shirt of Ed Cavanagh's, he thought. He got rid of the wet one and replaced it with the dry garment.

Meanwhile he tried to guess at the time when Craddock would reach the valley. Assuming that he would start down the creek trail soon after the hour when he was to be summoned, having to ride slowly in the darkness, it seemed probable that he would reach the homestead claims pretty close to daybreak. Undoubtedly Mitchell and his gang had planned it that way. Now that their scheme had failed they would be fully aware that time was running out on them. If they had Craddock on their necks while hostile witnesses still lived they would have failed, finally and fatally.

To Kendrick it meant that he had to anticipate a last deadly assault. Now that matters had gone so far, Mitchell wouldn't dare hold back. Perhaps he was waiting to lull the defenders into overconfidence before making the final desperate gamble.

The waiting became almost unbearable. Kendrick remained at his post in the doorway most of the time but occasionally moved completely around the house so as to listen on all sides. Nothing was stirring.

Finally he could begin to see the outline of the crag country. It was no more than a vague silhouette but it meant dawn, a wet dawn that would appear without much warning. Now the attack would have to come.

Almost with the thought he heard gunshots again, a few widely spaced shots that suggested a new kind of fight. His first thought was that Mitchell had ambushed Craddock to keep him from learning the truth but then he realized that the shooting had not come from the right direction. Someone was fighting along the lower creek.

15

THE drizzling rain ceased entirely while Kendrick listened to the scattering fire which he believed to be a running fight. Dawn was coming on quite definitely now and it was possible to make out familiar outlines near the house. This would have to be the time for that final assault that the rustlers simply had to make. Further delay would make their prospects hopeless.

Ten minutes passed and he began to wonder about the meaning of that last outbreak of shooting. Had Mac tried to break through? Was it possible that he had slipped through the enemy lines and had escaped so that they now knew it would be impossible to cover their actions?

Kendrick moved along the wall of the cabin so as to study each part of the valley which the half light permitted him to see but the scanning told him nothing. The other cabin was silent, no one moving near it.

Another ten minutes elapsed and there was still no move from the enemy. Relieved but puzzled, Kendrick went around the cabin again, this time seeing a few things he had been unable to make out earlier. There were three riderless horses along the base of the eastern highland. What appeared to be dead bodies could be seen beyond the corral and at a distance south of the other cabin. He felt reasonably sure of three but believed there were at least three more. But where were the live ones? Somebody had been doing a lot of shooting.

He was tempted to stir up a show of action by heading across for a check on Mac Smith but before he could make up his mind to take the risk there was an interruption. Two riders broke out of the trees a half mile up the creek. Craddock and Neal, he thought; now he had to sit tight and see what the next enemy move would be.

The two men were heading straight for the cabin he had been defending so he slipped back inside the doorway to wait. Almost at once he heard riders coming across from the southwestern edge of the valley. Neither Craddock nor Neal seemed to be alarmed so Kendrick held his post, waiting with the rifle in his hands and his six-gun stuck in his belt.

When the NA men were still a few yards beyond the corral he saw three men angle past the corner of the cabin to meet them. Two of the riders were strangers to him but the third was Amos Trappe. None of them turned to look toward him. Whether they knew of his presence or not he could not guess.

At that moment Craddock saw the bodies of the men who had been killed in the fight near the corral. He pulled up suddenly, his words to Neal not loud enough for Kendrick to hear. The whiskery man swung in front of him, his hand on his gun, and Kendrick saw that Neal was indeed the fellow who had been wounded in the cattle-killing raid. He was evidently favoring his left arm but not enough to hamper his movements very much.

"Glad you got here in a hurry," Trappe called loudly, pretending to ignore the show of belligerence. "It looks like you've been victimized by your own men."

"How is that?" Craddock asked, staring worriedly as he pulled his bronc to a halt.

"Your own men have been stealing your stock," Trappe replied easily. "I got information on it yesterday afternoon. A man I can't name slipped me the word that Floyd Mitchell and some of your other hands have been running a regular cattle business of their own on the side, blaming rustlers for the losses that they'd caused with their thievery."

"That's not the way I . . . " Craddock was obviously at a loss and Trappe took his time about breaking in on the unfinished protest.

"They had a good story worked out for you, Mr. Craddock. Things had got a bit tight for them so they planned to lay the blame on a couple of men who recently came into the valley. They drove some of your stock down here so it would be found on this property. Then they planted

120

your friend Neal here to pass you a false report that they were chasing rustlers. It was timed so you'd get here just after they'd killed the two men they wanted to accuse. No one would be alive to call them liars and there'd be cattle in the valley that would make it look as though thieves had brought them here."

Just as he finished the statement there was a single gunshot. The outraged Dave Neal had started to pull his gun as the meaning of Trappe's statement began to sink in. One of the riders at Trappe's shoulder beat him to the draw, shooting him out of the saddle.

"That was foolish of him," Trappe said judicially. "We had him dead to rights, of course, but he didn't have a chance of breaking away now. And it would have been handier to have him alive to talk!"

No one seemed to doubt that Neal had been dead before he hit the ground. Kendrick knew better than to doubt. Now he could see the game Amos Trappe was playing. In a way it was the same one Mitchell had tried. A good big lie could be very effective if there was no one around to call it a lie.

Craddock was still speechless and Trappe proceeded with his story, making it sound pretty good. "I took a hand partly to save innocent men and partly because I felt obligated," he said smoothly. "Mitchell's been selling me some of that stolen beef and taking payment in things like ammunition and gear. I figured he was taking stuff that would go to the ranch but it looks like it was mostly for his gang. Anyway I got the tip about his game tonight so I routed out a couple of my men and we rode over here just in time to take a hand."

"Where's Mitchell now?" Craddock demanded, finding his voice at last.

Trappe shrugged. "I haven't had a chance to find out. We've been doing a lot of fighting in the dark, mostly banging away when they jumped us. It just got light and we've been trying to locate the rest of the gang."

"Then it's time we took steps to find out a few things!" the Englishman snapped, his face bleak.

Kendrick had remained out of sight during the exchange, hearing it all but not quite knowing what to do about it. It looked to him as if Amos Trappe had tried to improve on Mitchell's bloody plans, hoping to exterminate his old henchmen after letting them get rid of the troublesome newcomers. Probably Trappe didn't yet know whether he had succeeded completely but he was playing it boldly. The killing of Neal had been done so cleverly that it had appeared to be self-defense but it was certain that Trappe had planned to get rid of the bearded outlaw. Neal couldn't have been allowed to talk any more than any of the other gang members.

Kendrick considered swiftly. If he spoke up immediately he'd run the chance of being gunned down by one of those hard faced men backing Trappe. On the other hand, what could he gain by more delay? It seemed like a good bet that Trappe still didn't know the truth about the Kendrick-Cavanagh mix-up. Otherwise there would be no point in his attempt to make this new move.

The only move seemed to be a bold one—so he made it. Stepping out into the gray morning he called, "Don't make any moves! I been getting shot at long enough. Just declare yourselves or make tracks!"

For an instant he thought he'd guessed wrong. Trappe's companions wheeled apart, cold menace in both hard faces.

Then Trappe snapped a harsh order. "No more shooting! This man's all right." After that he raised his voice to call out, "Glad to see you're still alive, Cavanagh. I thought maybe these polecats had cut you down before we could get here. Where's your partner?"

"Mac was in the other cabin," Kendrick told him coolly. "I hope he's been taking good care of himself."

Trappe nodded and burst forth with another account of how he had risked everything to foil the dirty plans of Floyd Mitchell and the other NA renegades. It was the same story he had just told Craddock but he went through it again, adding a few details which seemed to give it additional substance. He mentioned that he had become suspicious of Mitchell when he stumbled upon that hidden cattle trail in the high country.

It was cleverly done. Trappe was explaining everything which pointed to his own guilt, making each point

122

seem like a matter he had known nothing about. He had built up a pretty good case for himself, particularly if there was no one left alive to deny any part of the yarn.

There was a distant hail just as Trappe skimmed through the last of the story and Kendrick stole a sidelong glance to see Mac Smith coming out of the other cabin. That helped. Now there were two witnesses to the night's attack.

Kendrick felt some of the finely drawn tension drain out of him. He had condemned himself for letting Smith get into this deadly business but now he could ease his conscience. And there was added safety. Trappe couldn't afford another murder unless he figured to kill three men. Kendrick didn't think he'd risk cutting Craddock down.

"Looks like both of us pulled through," he said briefly, jerking a thumb toward the distant Smith. "With your help." As long as he was going to play Trappe's game, he might as well go the whole hog.

The trader's glance was searching but he seemed satisfied. "We did our best," he said gruffly.

Craddock intervened, horror and concern reflected in his polished accents. "We must take immediate steps to ascertain the nature of the casualties," he exclaimed. "There must be wounded men needing attention, outlaws though they may be."

"Let's go," Trappe said shortly.

Craddock could have saved himself the humane concern. A careful search of the valley disclosed eight dead bodies in addition to that of Dave Neal. The three men who had fallen in the fight with Kendrick were identified as NA riders. So were two others near the small cabin. Floyd Mitchell and Dusty Gower had fallen some distance to the south. Near them was a man whom Craddock refused to identify.

There was an uneasy stir between Trappe's henchmen but neither of them spoke. "Outside man for the rustlers, I suppose," Trappe said shortly. "Likely they had plenty of others hooked up with them. Maybe this one sold their stuff down the creek."

Kendrick did not comment but he noted the quick

looks exchanged between Trappe's hands. He thought he knew what they had in mind.

"Nine dead!" Craddock murmured, the full horror of it just beginning to dawn on him. "This is a terrible thing. We'll have to get into touch with the law and make a full report."

"We'll send word," Trappe growled unconcernedly. "Fights like this don't get much notice in this country. Mostly the lawmen are glad to have things cleaned up without them having to take a hand."

"But nine deaths can't be shrugged off—even in this country! I must insist on a full legal report. After all, eight of these fellows were my employes. I want the proper authorities to pass judgment."

"Might take a long time," Trappe told him. "Dead bodies don't keep good in this climate. I'd say we'd better bury them and send along our report to the law. It ought to be easy enough to figure out how it happened."

Kendrick was beginning to realize that he had seriously underestimated Trappe. The trader seemed to have everything figured out neatly, even at a time when he was skating on mighty thin ice.

When no one commented Trappe went on quickly. "I see it like this. Pick me up if I get it wrong anywhere along the line. Mitchell divided his gang so as to jump both cabins at the same time. That was part of his plan; he wanted the fights to be over long before Neal could bring Mr. Craddock down here. In the fight by the corral Cavanagh knocked over three of the raiders. Here by the little cabin Smith got two more. Am I right so far?"

Kendrick and Smith both nodded agreement. Kendrick knew that there was at least one hole in his part of the story and he suspected that Mac was likewise overlooking something. Dusty Gower's position was not accounted for.

"Right," Trappe repeated with clear satisfaction. "So Mitchell pulled back after that and while he was trying to decide on his next move he heard us coming up the creek. He couldn't afford to be caught at what he was doing so he came over to take a crack at us, hoping to catch us by surprise. But we knew what we were getting

124

into so we took care of ourselves. We know we killed one man then.

"After that things quieted down and we tried to scout the valley, wondering what had happened up to that point. There was a long lull and then two riders came at us again. We shot 'em both down. My guess is that Mitchell was one of the last pair. After that nothing happened until you and Neal showed up." He was talking directly to Craddock now. "You already know about how Neal tried to gun his way out when he learned that we knew of the plot."

Craddock nodded miserably. If he saw anything wrong with that reconstruction of the affair he didn't indicate it. Trappe looked sharply at Kendrick. "See anything wrong with the way I sized it up, Cavanagh?" he demanded.

Kendrick shrugged. "It could be just that way for all I could see. I know how it went at the corral but the rest was just gunshots in the night."

"Smith?"

The little man had taken his cue. "I suppose I killed that pair by the cabin. At least I was sure trying. For the rest of it I'm like Tom."

Trappe was finding it hard to conceal his triumph now. He issued orders to his henchmen, practically ignoring Craddock as he arranged to clear the little battlefield. Kendrick and Smith helped with the grisly chore and by noon the dead men were decently buried on a little rise above the clump of willows where the rustler trail came down to the creek.

"A real proper boothill for 'em," Trappe said with a nasty grin. "It was finding this trail that first made me suspicious of 'em in the first place."

Nobody commented. For the past couple of hours Trappe had been doing the talking for everybody. For Kendrick and Smith the silence was simply a matter of avoiding talk while letting Amos Trappe enlarge on his neatly contrived story. There had been no chance for any lengthy confidences between the two men but they understood each other well enough. They were going to let Trappe have plenty of rope. Unfortunately he used his rope cleverly, never entangling himself in it but instead strengthening his false position until it sounded entirely too good.

Craddock was silent in a different sort of way. Undoubtedly he was blaming himself for letting a situation get so bad that it had developed into such stark tragedy. He was pale and obviously shaken, his only comment being a frank statement to Kendrick as they finished burying the dead men. "Sorry if I seem more concerned about these dead men than I do about the injury they brought upon you—but they were my men and I thought well of them. I feel guilty about not believing you the other day; we might have saved some lives if I had known the truth."

Trappe's gunmen, a lanky, lantern-jawed young fellow called Spike and a shorter, more compact man named Haney, were no more talkative than the rest. They obeyed orders but they grumbled to each other and once Kendrick overheard Haney arguing sharply with Trappe, apparently about the unidentified corpse. Trappe won the argument but his backers became increasingly sullen as the morning progressed.

Finally Trappe suggested that Craddock go with him to Packsaddle. "You'll want to get that report filed," he pointed out. "They won't need you at the ranch right away and it'll be important for you to pick up some new hands in a hurry. I think I can help you out. I've got men coming in for some other work but I won't need them for quite a while. Maybe we can find some cow hands among them."

He paid little attention to Kendrick and Smith until he actually started to leave. Then he rode across to where they were sitting their horses, his words addressed to the vacant space between them. "Glad I could give you boys a hand," he said with a spurious benevolence. "But you'd better not depend on me being around for future rescues."

"You mean there's more trouble brewing?" Kendrick asked.

"Who knows?" The shrug was elaborately careless. "I've got an idea there's a hoodoo on this place. Eleven men killed around here in less than a year. It seems like a bad place to bet on. A couple of salty hombres like you should be able to do better somewhere else. I might even put you on to something good myself. Let me know if you get the notion to move on."

"We'll do that," Kendrick promised, his voice flat.

16

A FEW lingering white clouds were bright in the noonday sun when Kendrick and Smith rode back toward the small cabin. Looking at the greening valley now it was hard to believe that there had been so much violence and treachery here within the past few hours. Common sense rebelled at accepting the knowledge. The two men maintained an uneasy silence.

The spell was broken as they reached the cabin and Smith swung out of the saddle. "I'm figuring to take a nap," he announced. "A night like that takes a lot out of a man."

"Might as well join you," Kendrick agreed. "We're not out of the woods yet but I don't imagine we'll be getting jumped again today. By the way, how did you know Trappe was lying? Was it something to do with Dusty?"

"Sure. I figure Trappe and his sidekicks just plain massacred that poor fool."

"Want to tell me about your end of the brawl? I can guess at part of it but I'd like to know the whole story."

"I'd moved into the cabin when the rain started but I stuck around the door to listen. After a spell I heard a horse moving around out there in the dark but while I was trying to locate him I heard a gun bust out into a real rat-a-tat-tat. What did you do, fan 'em?"

Kendrick grinned feebly. "It seemed like a good way to declare war on an enemy I couldn't see too well."

Smith nodded. "Right after that I heard somebody yell over near the creek and then a horse broke into a gallop. Sounded like somebody from here was hustling over to find out what had happened on your end."

127

"Floyd Mitchell. I yelled at him in hopes that I might scare off any more attacks. I thought he might pull out if he knew his game was wide open. It was about then that I heard shots over here."

"Right. Two jaspers moved in on me and I cut one of them down right away. The other ducked out, yelling for Mitchell. A little later they tried to sneak in on me from the other side but I drove them off. After that things got real quiet so I decided to let Dusty loose. He'd told us the truth and I figured he might persuade the others to give up the job. Anyway, I let him go—unarmed—and knew that he'd got his horse clear of the corral. He seemed to head straight south—and then more firing busted out. My guess is that he ran into Trappe's gang and got gunned down without ever knowing what hit him."

"How many men moved in on you when the next big strike started?"

"None. I heard a man out there moving around just before things got hot at your position. I didn't shoot at him, though. Somebody else started to bang away so I just played shady and watched. Never saw a thing."

"I think Mitchell left one man to watch you while the survivors tried to blast me out. Trappe not only picked off the guard here but he caught the rest of the NA crowd when they tried to slip away, gunning down wounded like the rest. Probably Mitchell was the last one to get it. I knew he was lying about being in a fight with the NA outfit. At least one of them wasn't looking for any more fights when he got away from my post. Trappe and his men must have been burning them down wherever they found them, making sure nobody could do any talking."

"Sounds that way. What about the odd man that Craddock didn't claim?"

"One of Trappe's gang, I think. The last couple of NA men put up a fight."

"But why didn't Trappe claim him and take him away as a dead hero? That might have been a smart move if Trappe is figuring to play the part he was talking so big."

Kendrick shook his head. "I don't understand that part

128

—and neither did those two thugs Trappe had with him. They didn't like it."

"We'll not worry about it," Smith said with a wry grin. "None of 'em was any loss. 'I am no mourner . . . They have still been mine enemies'." Then he added with a very good imitation of Mr. Glass's slightly inebriated pomposity, *"Richard the Third."*

The unexpectedness of the quotation and the mimicry broke the tension. Kendrick chuckled. "We're rid of a fine collection of enemies but we can't do any crowing. Trappe didn't pull this neat little massacre for our benefit."

"You figure he still plans to get rid of us?"

"Likely. My guess is that he expected Mitchell to get rid of us and then he would do the same for Mitchell. When he found that only half of his plan was working he was smart enough to make a quick change in it, coming up with this rescue story."

"It's a hard story to bust," Smith growled. "He explains every little thing to suit his own purpose. Do you think he's still worried about us?"

"He passed a pretty strong hint that he wanted us to light a shuck. If we don't accept the advice he'll probably make a new move. Maybe he won't be in any hurry, but he'll do something sooner or later. He's got to put some kind of pressure on Jo to work things out his own way and he won't want us around when the time comes for the big gamble."

"Then we'd better get ready. He talked like he was bringing in extra men, most likely for the wood-cutting chores—and if they're anything like the pair he had with him this morning they'll be tough hombres!"

The peacefulness of the afternoon had been just as marked in Packsaddle as it had been out at the valley homesteads. There had been a brief flurry when Trappe and Craddock rode in with the news of the night battle but after that the excitement died away rapidly. A few casual strollers passed their comments on the news but at Trappe's trading post very little was happening. Craddock paused in town only long enough to get a fresh horse and a meal, then he rode on down the valley in search of some arm of the law. Neither Trappe nor his hard faced men showed up again during the afternoon.

The soft spring evening was still mellowed by the rosy glow behind the western ranges when Jo and her father reached town, the girl dismounting in evident weariness before the Assay Office. "I'll go in and rest a little," she told her father in a tired voice. "Ask Amos if he'll come over here as soon as he can make it. I'd prefer not to go into his place just now and I think we should get on the trail of this mystery as soon as we can manage."

The little man nodded wearily. Two hard days of riding had taken a lot out of him. "Amos will know what to do, my dear," he assured her. "Go in and make yourself comfortable. It may be that he'll not be able to come along for a few minutes. He's a business man, you know."

"I'll wait," she replied. "Anything to get clear of that infernal saddle for a while."

She was stumbling toward the building as she spoke, only half aware that her father had ridden on down the street. Two days of that saddle! And for what? Only to find out that Ramirez didn't believe Tom was dead! How stupid could people get?

She did not bother to light a lamp but went straight to an old leather sofa which had been part of the early furniture of the place, back in the days before her marriage. It was sheer luxury to stretch out on it and some of her sense of humor returned. An hour ago she would have declared that she never wanted any contact with leather again. But this was different.

For the better part of an hour she was content to take her ease but then the fatigue began to drain out of her and worry came back. Why hadn't her father returned? Why didn't Amos Trappe come? What caused the mysterious attitude of that clerk in Cimarron?

Going to the door she stared out into the night but there was nothing to be seen. Yellow rectangles of light marked a few nearby houses or stores and there was a greater glow down the street where Amos Trappe's place stood. The town seemed peaceful enough but somehow it seemed to be an uneasy peace that filled the night. She told herself that she was imagining things just because she was tired and because her plans had gone awry—but the feeling persisted.

She waited another half hour. Still nothing happened. Amos should have come along by this time. At least her father should have sent some word. She knew there had been a certain amount of risk in exposing the Glass thirst to the temptations of the Trading Post bar but she had hoped for better luck. Now she decided that she might have to take firmer steps.

She moved back to the door again, this time stepping out into the night. A man came toward her from the direction of Trappe's place, his long shadow almost grotesque against the irregular lights. He limped heavily on his left leg but he was moving fast.

She had half a mind to go back out of sight until he passed but then she heard him call out, "That you, Mrs. Kendrick? Mind if I have a word with you?" The voice sounded young, almost excited.

"Is it about my father?" she asked, a sudden dread striking hard at her.

"Not exactly, ma'am." He was close now, halting where a distant light brought his features into shadowy clarity. A tall young fellow with a crooked leg. "I was talkin' to your pappy for quite a spell and somehow what he told me don't fit out right."

"He has been drinking then?"

"Some. But not enough to get things muddled up the way they seem. I headed down into this country to find a man named Kendrick. I heard he got married and then soon after got killed. I was about to move on but then I heard that Kendrick's wife was still in the country. So I decided to wait and meet you. That was only this afternoon, I oughta tell you. Now I get some kind of story about Tom gettin' killed away last winter some time."

"That's exactly correct," she replied, wondering what he was getting at. "My husband was killed by outlaws last February."

"And he was Tom Kendrick? Corporal Tom Kendrick of the Third Cavalry, Troop L?"

"Of course!" She snapped the reply a little more posi-

131

tively than she really felt. A suspicion was beginning to gnaw at her. Ever since those two men came into the valley and acted so strangely about everything she had been uneasy over the whole situation. Now the Land Office at Cimarron seemed to be throwing out some questions. Finally this stranger was hinting along the same line.

"I don't see how it could work that way, ma'am," the man said worriedly. "I was in Tom Kendrick's squad at the Rosebud fight. I got hurt real bad in the first skirmish. Later in the hospital I heard that Kendrick was killed. Still later they told me he'd showed up in fairly good shape."

"That is the story of my husband," she said simply.

"But it can't be. Kendrick never got back to the fort till late last fall. He'd been hurt so much the Injuns had to take care of him all summer. Then he was at the post for the winter while the army untangled his lost records. I got it straight from an officer who was with him most of the winter. Tom Kendrick didn't leave Fort Russell, Wyoming, until March. It just ain't possible that he got killed down here in February."

She studied him in a cold silence for several seconds. It was not easy to make herself calm but she knew that she had to do it. This man was honestly disturbed. She had to talk to him as intelligently as possible, making herself forget that icy despair which seemed to be gnawing at her.

"Who are you that you should come here with such a story?" she asked.

"My name is Michaels, ma'am. I was in Tom Kendrick's squad."

"Was there a man named Cavanagh in that squad?"

"No, ma'am. Ed Cavanagh was platoon sergeant."

"What about a man named Smith?"

"Mac Smith? The Shakespeare fiend? Sure. Him and Kendrick and me are all that's left of the squad. Or maybe it's only Mac and me—if Kendrick is gone now."

"Do you have a horse handy?"

"Yes, ma'am."

"Get it and come back here as fast as you can. I think

132

it's time to get this thing settled once and for all. We'll give you a chance to name some names."

Amos Trappe had not spent a very pleasant afternoon with his hired gunmen. Both Spike and Haney had complained bitterly about the way he had let poor Warner be buried with those NA corpses.

"It's no way to treat a man who done all he could," Haney insisted. "We coulda brought him back here and buried him decent. As long as we're settin' ourselves up as a bunch of damned heroes we might as well have a dead hero to show folks. Kinda get sympathy, it would."

Trappe shrugged. "Warner's dead. What difference does it make to him where he gets planted?"

"It still ain't decent treatment!" Spike cut in. "I ain't no better than lots of others that sell theirselves as fightin' men but I kinda like to figure I'm workin' fer a man who won't throw me down if I stop a slug. Maybe I get killed—so it's all part of the business—but I'd like to know I get treated decent if it happens." He was almost whining.

"You're a pair of damned idiots!" Trappe snapped. "I had a good reason for not claiming Warner's carcass. Nobody but us knew he was around here so there won't be anybody askin' questions. Instead we let that Limey get the idea that his boys had some outside help. So now we pass the word that there might be another half dozen men in the gang."

"What good does that do?"

"Look. Sooner or later we've got to clean up the job Mitchell blundered on. I've got an idea that Smith and Cavanagh won't take my advice to move. So I've got to get rid of them before I start pushing for a final settlement with the widow. If both of them get ambushed some bright morning we can always let word get around that the rustler survivors came back to get even with them for killing Mitchell and the others."

Haney nodded his understanding. "I see. If we hadn't left Warner with the rest of 'em it might look like there wasn't no more rustlers. Right?"

"Right. Now see if you can't make Spike understand."

133

"I understand all right," the younger man growled. "When do we cut loose on them boys up the crick?"

"Easy," Trappe cautioned. "We'll let this simmer down a bit. A little talk here and there ought to build up the idea that somebody might still have it in for Cavanagh and Smith—maybe even for Mrs. Kendrick and her old man. In a couple of days we'll figure out something. Then we clean house."

"Just us?"

"Sure. I don't want any dumb woodcutters in on a deal like this one. You boys can handle it—and the split will be bigger for you."

Finally the gunmen agreed to go along. By that time darkness had fallen and the first stirrings of evening business sounded from the bar.

"We'll get out there now and talk it up," Trappe told them. "Strut a bit. Play the hero right up to the hilt. We've got to convince everybody."

They went into the bar as casually as possible but Trappe lost his fine air of ease at sight of the white haired man who hung by his elbows on the mahogany. Old Glass hadn't been on a drunk like this one in many weeks.

Trappe went to him quickly, trying to get him away from the bar. Glass refused to budge. "A weary man doth need his refreshment," he intoned thickly. "I'll drink no more than will do me good." The red face turned up a pleased smile as he explained in a whisper, "That last part is from *Henry the Fourth*. The first part I don't know about; maybe I made it up myself."

"When did you get back?" Trappe asked.

"Hour, maybe. I rode right over to get you to . . . " He shook his head as though puzzled by his own perplexity. "Musta been something I was goin' to . . . Alas, as somebody says in *Othello*, 'I have very poor and unhappy brains for drinking.' But there was some reason. I know there was."

"Where's Jo?" Trappe asked roughly.

"I don't remember. Can't seem to remember much of anything since I got to talkin' with that . . . that boy who

134

claimed he knew Kendrick. Crazy fellow, claimed Kendrick was still alive!"

Trappe swung to face the bartender. "Did you hear anybody talking about Kendrick?"

The man in the apron nodded. "Sure. Young sprout. Said he'd been in the army with Kendrick and wanted to see him. Seemed all put out when I told him Kendrick was dead."

"What else did he say?"

"I didn't hear nothin' else. Old Empty came in about that time and downed about five quick ones. I left the kid talkin' to him and went on about my business."

"Crazy kid," Glass muttered, having a hard time to stay on his feet as the series of quick drinks built up a cumulative effect. "Said Tom alive up in Wyoming about a month ago."

Trappe nodded toward his henchmen and they hustled Glass around toward the rear room. "Looks like we can't wait a couple of days," Trappe said. "I've got a feeling I made a bad mistake. One we've got to do something about in a hurry."

17

THE afternoon passed quickly for Kendrick and Smith. The little man had to hear the full explanation of Kendricks's theory about the timber and the telling involved a detailed account of the trip to Cimarron. They talked while they caught up with their chores and repaired the negligible fight damage. At the smaller cabin there were three bullet holes in the door and a number of other slugs in the log wall near it but at the Hockett place the only real damage was to the unused rain barrel. Three slugs had gone through it, leaving six more or less splintered holes.

Shortly before dusk Smith caught up with some of his

sleeping. By that time both men were red-eyed from the long hours of vigilance and conflict but Kendrick was in no mood for a nap. He knew that he had to make plans. Trappe would be back.

At nightfall he made supper, waking Mac only when the meal was ready. "It looks like Jo and the old man won't come back tonight," he remarked. "Probably they'll use three days for the round trip to Cimarron. That means we'll have to stand guard tonight, just in case Trappe decides to take a crack at us while we're here alone. It could be a lot simpler for him if he doesn't have to figure around the others—and he'll be just the lad to take such an angle into account."

"Sounds likely," Mac agreed. "Do you figure we ought to stay here and wait to see what happens?"

Kendrick shrugged. "Probably. We've got the property to protect just as much as we did before. Anyway it's as good a place to defend as any."

"Suits me. I'll take the first watch. I had a nap already."

Kendrick did not argue. He crawled into his bedroll while Smith took over the clean-up chores, dropping off to sleep immediately. His final thought was that there was one factor in their favor; Trappe and his gunmen had also lost a night of sleep so maybe they would not be in a hurry to start another brawl.

It seemed to him that he had scarcely closed his eyes when Mac was shaking him. "Better get up, Tom," the little man said quietly. "I've been outside and I just heard a couple of riders coming up the creek. I already blew out the lamp."

"Just two?" Kendrick asked, getting his legs under him in a hurry. "That could be Jo and her father coming back."

"Not likely. I don't figure they'd travel in the dark and anyway this pair seems to be headed straight at our cabin and not across toward the other one."

They were almost at the door as he spoke. Kendrick grunted agreement and added, "Take the west corner and I'll take the east. Keep a bit of log in front of you no matter which way they close in. Let me do the talking while we figure out what it means."

"Yes, Corporal Kendrick." Mac chuckled dryly as he moved away.

They separated in the starlit night and Kendrick hurried around to the corner he had picked for himself, listening to the hoofbeats that were now so close. The intruders were walking their horses, making no attempt at stealth, but he realized that it might be a ruse. Maybe they hoped to get close simply by appearing careless.

The dark forms showed in the gloom then and he knew that his ears had not deceived him. There were two of them out there. He waited until the outlines were sharp enough to make good targets and then he called sternly, "Hold it right there! Now speak up. Who are you and what do you want?"

There was a faint gasp of dismay but then a familiar voice replied, "It's Jo. Is something wrong?"

"Who's with you? Your father?"

"No. . . . It's not Father."

"Then who is it?" Kendrick's voice took on a note of greater urgency. "We're taking no chances around here tonight. I want to know who it is!"

"Trust me," the girl said in an odd voice. "You'll understand soon enough."

"All right. Move in slowly. I'll have a gun on him every second." He had not relaxed for an instant and his tone said so. After having witnessed Amos Trappe's style of treachery he couldn't afford to take needless risks.

Jo said something in a low voice to her companion and the dark blurs moved forward again. When they were ten feet away Kendrick ordered, "Get down, both of you. Jo, you take both horses around to the hitch rack—and make sure that you don't get in my line of fire."

"You're certainly being dramatic," she snapped, her tone impatient. "What in the world has happened out here?"

"You didn't hear about it?"

"No. What was it?"

"A pitched battle that lasted all night. I'll tell you about it later."

"Is Mac all right?"

"Sure. We were both real lucky—and we're trying to

make sure that the luck doesn't run out. Get those horses moved around."

He waited until she had cleared the corner and then he snapped an order at the waiting stranger. "Start moving, mister. Right around the cabin. I'm right behind you with a cocked gun."

"You're the boss, Corporal," the man said unexpectedly. "I'm not here for trouble so don't squeeze that trigger." His voice sounded vaguely familiar but Kendrick could not recognize either the lean shadow or the limping gait.

They reached the cabin door just as Mac came up from the other side. "That's far enough," Mac cut in. "We'll hold it here while the lady takes care of her chore."

"Go inside and strike a light," Jo called. "I'm right behind you."

Mac led the way and presently the bracket lamp over the kitchen table sprang into yellow life. Kendrick blinked in surprise at sight of his prisoner but it was Smith who spoke, softly but with a ring of astonishment. "Damned if it isn't the boy hero of Troop L!"

Jo interrupted hastily. "Don't say another word, please! I want to be sure. Mr. Michaels, will you name these two men?"

The young fellow was grinning in mixed pleasure and embarrassment. "Sorry if I busted into something, gents, but . . ."

"Name them!" Jo snapped, her tone wholly grim now.

"Go ahead," Kendrick told him. "We might as well get everything clear."

Michaels grinned a bit sheepishly and nodded. "Like I said, ma'am, this jasper is Tom Kendrick who couldn't have got hisself killed here in February because he didn't leave Wyoming 'til March. The sassy little rascal is ole Shakespeare Smith."

The girl seemed to slump. "What does it all mean?" she exclaimed. "If this is Tom Kendrick, who was my husband? And who does it make me?"

"Better sit down," Kendrick advised. "We've got to talk it out the long way so we might as well be comfortable."

A faint humor broke through her distress. "I'll stand.

138

After what seems like six months in the saddle there is no enticement in the idea of sitting."

Kendrick chuckled dryly. "Have it your own way but tell me one thing first. Does Amos Trappe know about Michaels?"

"Why?"

"Does he? Answer the question!"

Michaels answered it. "I reckon he does, Corp. I spent quite a bit of time tryin' to get this Kendrick yarn untangled and a lot of people heard what I had to say. I didn't talk to anybody named Trappe but I got the idea from the lady that Trappe kinda runs the roost back where I was doin' my talkin'. Chances are he's smarted up to the deal by now."

"How many men does he have in Packsaddle now?"

Michaels shook his head. "Didn't seem like many. I got into town in the middle of the afternoon and I was around Trappe's place quite a spell. I heard that Trappe and a couple of his non-coms are spendin' the afternoon in a council-of-war. There didn't seem to be anybody else around exceptin' the bartender, a store clerk and a couple of old characters at the stable."

"What difference does it make?" Jo demanded. "What does it matter who is working for Amos Trappe? I want to know . . ."

"We'll get to it in a jiffy," Kendrick promised her. "The point right now is that your friend Mr. Trappe has been running a mighty nasty game around here. He managed to get nine men killed here last night—and I'm not figuring to let him add the four of us to his total."

"No," Smith said soberly. "That would make thirteen. An unlucky number—particularly if you're one of the thirteen."

The girl's confusion was now complete. The fact that Smith was making a grim joke in the face of danger did not register with her at all. The shock of what she had just learned, along with the hints at further disclosures, was a little too much.

Kendrick spoke quickly, realizing how she must feel. "Take some blankets out by the back corner," he told Smith. "We'll let Jo stretch out on the ground while we fill in the holes in the story. That way she can rest her saddle blisters and we'll be able to keep our ears open while we get our talking done."

It took a lot of talking. Kendrick did most of it with Smith putting in an occasional word of explanation, Jo and Michaels asking questions when they could not follow the complicated pattern of events. At first the girl seemed resentful and bitter but then her tone began to change. The grim logic of the case Kendrick was outlining could not be denied.

Both Kendrick and Smith tried to ease her feelings by pointing out that Ed Cavanagh's offense had been an impersonal one. He hadn't tried to hurt anybody but had simply taken advantage of a situation. He would have considered his action much in the light of a man finding property to which no one had any real claim.

"But he did it knowing it was fraud," the girl said clearly. "He had to figure out a lot of things with Amos Trappe before he dared to make the claim."

"My guess is that Trappe was planning some kind of dirty deal for Ed once he had served his purpose in the Amos Trappe program. It stands to reason that Trappe didn't back him out of any kind motives. For one thing, Amos had ideas about marrying you so it wasn't likely that he felt real kindly toward the man who had come into the valley and spoiled his ambitions. For another thing, Amos wanted this property so he could claim that timber and at the same time protect the operations of his thieving partners at NA. I think he pretended to string along with Ed partly as a blind for what he was planning to do next.

"Then Ed got my letter and knew that his game was up. He must have hinted to Trappe that he was thinking of getting out—although it's a cinch he didn't tell Trappe why. So Amos moved first, sending his rustler pards on one of those raids like the one in which Uncle Bill was killed. For Trappe that would have seemed to clear the way."

Smith chuckled dryly. "But then you got nosey and picked up the trail of the rustlers."

"That's right—but Amos still didn't tumble to the fact

140

that the man who had exposed his game was a man who'd know other things about him. So far as he knew I was a stranger. He was willing to have Floyd Mitchell get rid of me. When Floyd failed on the job Trappe played the next best game. He decided to make it look as though Mitchell was the only villain of the show. If I'd been the stranger he took me for I might have been fooled."

"But now he knows," Jo said in a tight voice.

"Probably. Another man who was reported dead tipped him off."

"Sorry," Michaels growled. "I didn't know . . ."

"I'm not blaming you. Maybe it's just as well. Now we've got Trappe to the point of desperation. At this stage he may not be thinking as smart as he has been doing."

"What do you figure he'll do next?"

"That's the big question. I've been trying to put myself in Trappe's place, asking myself what I would do if I had his problem. . . . Suddenly I discover that a fellow I've thought of as a sort of impersonal nuisance is really a man who knows me and knows what I've been doing. I figure he's been playing cat and mouse with me. He can ruin every plan I've been making. He'll ruin them—if he gets the chance."

There was a brief pause before he went on, "So I know I have to try some more of my extermination program. There's no other way to salvage anything out of the wreckage. Kendrick—and Smith—have to go!"

Jo's voice broke in with a little more spirit. After the first shock of understanding she had started thinking again. "But he must know that you aren't keeping your secret alone. He certainly has heard about Michaels and he must know that I left Packsaddle with Michaels. Maybe he even suspects that you have told other people. Undoubtedly he knows that you went to Cimarron."

"Right enough," Kendrick agreed. "Now let me be Trappe again. I know those things you just mentioned. I can make the desperate attempt to kill off everybody who can spill the beans—just as I disposed of every man who could tell the truth about my connection with the NA rustlers. In that case there's a chance for me to brazen the whole thing through and depend on getting everything

I want through my partner. If the law can be fooled my partner will be heir to this property."

"But my father would not . . . " Jo interrupted.

"Your father would be easy to fool. He's no problem on this deal. The dubious point is at Cimarron. Has the law been notified of the fraud? If so there's more trouble. I—Trappe—identified Ed Cavanagh as Tom Kendrick when he made his claim to the property. Maybe I'm in more of a jam than I knew."

His voice altered swiftly as he flung a question at Michaels. "Did you meet a man named Craddock in Packsaddle today?"

"No. But I heard the name mentioned. Somebody said he'd gone down the crick to get a lawman. I didn't get the point of why he wanted one but I know now. He was dead set on reportin' this riot you had out here last night."

"Then Trappe knows he's pressed for time. If he's going to try any more desperation killing he's got to do it in a hurry. It'll be too late to make any moves like that if Craddock and the law appear on the scene. I think we'd better get set for trouble."

"Going to wait here?" Smith asked.

"Why not? We're better fixed to defend ourselves than we were last night—and we didn't do bad then. It's better than risking a move in the dark."

"I vote to stay," Jo said quietly. "I'm sure I couldn't ride any more tonight. But I can handle a gun."

"Get everything together," Kendrick directed. "We'll set our defenses at the big cabin. Don't leave anything here that we can't afford to lose if they decide to set fire to the place. Let's go; we've talked long enough."

"I'll walk over," Jo stated firmly.

"We'll all walk," Kendrick agreed with a dry chuckle. "Light skirmish order. Hit it up, First Squad!"

18

THE move to the Hockett cabin was made without delay or incident, Michaels the only one showing any signs of excitement. He, a newcomer, had run headlong into an unexpectedly dangerous and dramatic situation. For the others the danger was nothing new. Until tonight they hadn't understood the true nature of their peril but they had lived under a tension which had been almost as bad. Now that they awaited a climax it was no worse than the drawn-out tensions.

Kendrick took the first watch, admonishing the others to get as much sleep as possible. Maybe Trappe would strike early, hopeful of getting clear of the valley before daybreak. Maybe he would play Indian and gamble on the sleepy hour before dawn. Vigilance would be essential all the way.

It was shortly after eleven when the guard routine began, Kendrick walking a sentry beat that would cover all sides of the house as well as the corral. He felt certain that no one could approach from any direction across the open valley without being heard. Not that he anticipated any open approach by the enemy; Trappe was too smart for that.

He had made two complete circuits of the property when there was the soft scuff of feet near the back door of the cabin. He stopped in his tracks, halfway across the corral, and listened intently, afraid that he had been lax enough to let someone close in on the place. Then Jo's voice came in a cautious whisper:

"Mind if I join you? I can't sleep."

He moved toward her before replying, "You can help listen. Want to take a post or prowl along with me?"

"I'll prowl. Anything is better than sitting or lying down."

He grinned in the darkness. They moved silently

143

around the house, halting on the far side to listen as they faced the dangerous south.

"Still quiet," Kendrick whispered finally. "I'm beginning to think he won't risk it."

"Do you think he might try to use Father in some way?"

"Not likely. Your father is his last chance to make any part of his game look legal. We're the ones he has to get."

"I understand. It's not a happy thought. But what if he tries something else?"

"He can't have much choice. Yesterday he must have figured that he covered a lot of things when he got those NA men buried. Now he has to figure that Tom Kendrick helped to bury them—and Tom Kendrick would have been suspicious. Tom Kendrick would have noticed that at least two of them were shot in a number of places, gunned down to silence them after they were already wounded and out of the fight. Trappe has to take that into account."

She was silent while they made another complete round. When she spoke again it was in the same hushed whisper but there was a note of troubled wonder in her voice. "I'm just beginning to appreciate how you must have felt that morning when I told you I was Mrs. Tom Kendrick—a widow. What did you think at that moment?"

"I felt like Banquo's Ghost—if you don't mind Shakespeare slipping into the conversation again."

"I'm used to it. . . . At the moment I'm not sure who I am. I'm certainly not Mrs. Tom Kendrick—but who am I? Was I married to anyone?"

"No question on that score," he assured her. "You're the widow of a man named Edward Cavanagh. What he called himself when he married you doesn't affect the situation at all."

"And that sounds all the more confusing. I think of you as Cavanagh, of course."

"Sounds like you're determined to be my widow. Lucky I'm not superstitious."

"Please don't joke about it. It's rather horrible all around."

144

"Not entirely." Suddenly he had to tell her what had been in the back of his mind. "Some parts of all this have been very nice. If you hadn't been so determined on your role as dignified widow I'd have . . . "

"You don't need to be gallant, I haven't been hinting."

"I didn't take it that way—and I never sound gallant unless I mean it. Now you'd better get back to the cabin and rest a bit. Some time when you're not under so much strain we'll take up this other matter."

"Thanks for being kind. And please don't think me silly for bringing up the nonsense about my name."

"We'll fix it," he said with a chuckle. "Right now I'm just happy that you don't hold it against me that I deceived you."

"But you had no choice. I understand that."

"I could have told you at once. At first I wasn't sure of you. Then I didn't want to do anything that might make you leave."

She started away but flung back a whisper that did not sound quite as weary as her earlier words. "I think I understand. Good night—Tom."

Kendrick settled down determinedly. He had to stop thinking. He had to listen.

When he awakened Michaels an hour or so later there had been no sign of trouble. The young fellow crawled out promptly, listening to the soft snores from opposite ends of the cabin. "Sounds plumb peaceful," he muttered. "The lady's got her nerve, sleepin' like that."

Kendrick went out with him, taking a few minutes to make sure that the new sentry was wide awake and certain of his directions. "Be sure you keep an ear cocked toward both slopes as well as down the creek," he warned. "We're dealing with a tricky hombre."

"Don't worry about me," Michaels retorted. "I learned how to handle guard duty from the best non-com in Troop L."

"You mean Ed Cavanagh?"

"Aw, go to bed! No use tryin' to butter up a jasper like you!"

Kendrick went, smiling to himself, suddenly very glad that he had men like Michaels and Smith to back him.

145

In spite of his weariness sleep did not come easily but eventually he dropped off, waking to find daylight at the windows. Michaels was snoring loudly on the floor and a softer sound was coming from the bunk.

He slipped out without waking either of them and found Mac studying the distant willows down the creek. "Anything?" he asked.

"Nary a peep. Looks like we expected too much."

"It's just as well. Now what should we do?"

Mac grimaced. "Don't ask me. I'm just a high private in the rear rank. You're the board of strategy—you and Mrs. Whatever-her-name-is."

"All right. Get a fire going and start the coffee. While you're doing that I'll scout a bit. Then we'll hold a confab."

"Don't run into an ambush. Maybe it's what they're waiting for you to do." He chuckled as he added, "You've got to watch out—as they say in *Richard the Third*—for 'a thing devised by the enemy'."

"Get on the job—and 'save me so much talking!' That's from *Henry the Eighth,* by the way."

"You're contaminated!" Smith accused with a laugh. "So I'll say get on with your scouting. 'Tis shame for us all: so God sa' me; tis shame for to stand still.' *Henry the Fifth*." Then he almost ran for the door of the house.

Kendrick grinned briefly as he turned away, grimness returning as he swung wide to approach the valley outlet by way of the screening timbers. Logic told him that Trappe wasn't going to attack. Only a prompt and deadly assault would have done him any good and the time for it was past. Still it was necessary to guard against everything.

A half hour's search assured him that no enemies had come into the area during the night. He reported it that way when he returned to the cabin and found a hasty breakfast almost ready.

"Guessed wrong," he said shortly. "Anybody want to make a new prediction?"

Nobody did. Kendrick nodded gravely. "Then we take the offensive. Can you ride now, Jo?"

"Where?"

"To Packsaddle."

Smith cut in quickly. "Better leave her here, Tom. If we start any real ruckus it'll be better to have her in the clear."

"Bigger risk to leave her," Kendrick said shortly. "Maybe Trappe is hoping for something like that. The four of us stay together from now on. We can't afford to separate."

The point seemed clear to all of them and after a quick meal they saddled up and headed down the creek, Michaels and Jo riding the trail while Kendrick and Smith deployed as skirmishers on either slope. It wasn't quite staying together but it seemed like the thing to do.

The sun was up as they swung around the south shoulder of the east mountain, the day promising beautiful weather. Too nice a day to be going out to hunt trouble, Kendrick thought. He was on the left flank, having taken that post so he could check the hidden trail as they crossed it. Watching for sign was reasonably simple now; the rain of the previous night and morning had left the ground ready for any new marks. When he found none he felt pretty certain that there were really none to be found.

A half mile short of Packsaddle they joined forces, riding in a close knot as they discussed their chances. Trappe had definitely not made any attempt to strike at the homestead area. What was he planning to do?

Sight of the town gave them no hint. A few people were attending to their usual chores, no one appearing to have anything unusual in mind. Kendrick made a decision promptly. "The three of you hole up in the Assay office. I'll move in on Trappe's place."

"That's suicide!" Smith exclaimed.

"Simmer down. Killing me now won't get him anything; the rest of you obviously know the whole truth by this time so Trappe will realize that he can't gain anything by gunning me down. He's a first class thug at heart but he's a smart one; he doesn't kill unless he stands to gain by it."

"But be careful," Jo said anxiously.

He gave her a crooked grin. "I'm a real careful lad, Mrs. Blank."

He rode away while the others were dismounting to enter the little office. There was no one in sight around the trading post so he pushed right in, gun hand ready. Nothing happened. No one was at the bar or at any of the store counters.

The door to Trappe's office was partly open so he kicked it the rest of the way, gun in hand this time. If there was a deadfall set for him this would be it. Again nothing happened.

On a sofa against the wall Mr. Glass snored heavily, his white head hanging over the edge at a neck-breaking angle. Kendrick sniffed a couple of times and lifted the head to a more comfortable position. Then he moved across to the desk and stared down at a slip of paper on which a paragraph of hazy writing appeared. It was the carbon tracing of an agreement and it had been signed by Amos Trappe and Montgomery T. Glass, the signature of Mr. Glass looking somewhat stilted as though it had been laboriously traced. The paper recited that the partnership of Trappe and Glass had been dissolved, the parties agreeing to such dissolution with Glass taking title to all property then in the town known as Packsaddle, Trappe becoming sole owner of all funds and other assets of the company.

Kendrick read it twice, then went out at a run, this time seeing a man coming out of another back room. It was Trappe's bartender. He was barefooted and in his undershirt, looking heavy-eyed and annoyed but not at all worried.

"Didn't waste no time gettin' here, did you?" he greeted. "I don't have no more'n time to git to sleep after Amos leaves and right away somebody else is gallopin' through the place."

"Where's Trappe?" Kendrick demanded.

The bartender shrugged. "Gone. Cleared out. Skeedaddled! Him and them brush apes Haney and Spike."

"Gone for good?"

"Yep. Gone fer good. Amos told me he'd split the partnership, leavin' everything up here in the hills to ole

148

Empty." He grinned crookedly and jerked a thumb toward the office. "Is the old sponge still full? I hear him snorin' in there."

"Full as a tick," Kendrick replied. "Which way did Trappe go—and when?"

The bartender yawned. "Headed fer Raton Pass, I figure. Left about an hour ago. You think ole Empty will keep me on here?"

"Ask him when he wakes up. Anybody with Trappe except the two you mentioned?"

"Nope. Them two manure forkers at the stable might wish they'd gone along when they hear about it, though. Trappe took all the dinero out of the safe when he left so there ain't goin' to be no money to pay 'em off. I was on the spot and awake so I got paid." He seemed well pleased with himself.

Kendrick was out of the place before the man could say more, his first quick suspicions well verified. Trappe had out-guessed all of them. He swung into the saddle and spurred across toward the assayer's office, the three waiting people coming out to meet him while a half dozen casual observers turned to stare with open curiosity.

"I was stupid," he snapped. "All along I said that Trappe was smart, that he didn't kill unless he saw a chance to gain by it. Maybe I was so sure I was important to him that I didn't see the other things that balanced the scales. Anyway he made his choice and ducked out."

"You mean he threw everything to the winds?" Jo gasped. "Then where is my father?"

"Snoring," Kendrick told her shortly. "How much cash did your father have in this partnership?"

"Around six thousand dollars."

"Then it looks like Trappe has maybe won again. Last night he got your father to sign an agreement to split the partnership. The place here is now your father's property. Everything else belongs to Trappe, including all of the cash and securities he took with him. I suppose you could prove that your father was drunk when he signed the paper but finding Trappe to bring any suit against him won't be easy."

"We're well rid of him!" she exclaimed. "And maybe not with too much loss. The store and that machinery must be worth . . . "

"I'll bet precious little of it is paid for! If I know Trappe, he's left your father holding the bag for a lot of debts. He saw that the odds were going against him so he grabbed everything negotiable and skipped."

"You mean he has given up everything he killed to get?"

"That's the way it looks. He didn't hesitate to throw over the rustling game when he saw he couldn't hold on any longer. Now he knows he can't hope to get that timber land. So he's pulled out with whatever he could salvage. Maybe it's plenty and maybe it's not much—but it's more than he could hope to hold by sticking around."

He bent toward Michaels, reaching for the rifle the younger man had been carrying. "Give me that and a handful of shells," he ordered. "The rest of you stay here and see that nobody interferes with the new owner of the post. I think maybe I can stop Trappe before he gets clean away."

Jo grabbed the bridle of his horse. "Don't do it," she said, her voice low but intense. "Let him go. It will be worth something to be rid of all this killing."

Kendrick shook his head. "That's one reason I have to go. This killing has been Trappe's doing. Maybe he didn't pull the trigger on many of the victims but it was his work just the same. Eleven men have died here in less than a year. He's not going to get off scot free!"

He was stuffing shells into a pocket as he looked down at her, well aware of what he was reading in her eyes. "That's the way it has to be," he added.

"But it doesn't! You have everything you wanted here. It's not worth the risk. Revenge won't . . . "

"Look," he said. "You just don't know what this means to me. One of the things I dreamed about all the time I was up north was to come down here and give Uncle Bill a hand. I owed him that help. I wanted to pay my debt. It was Amos Trappe who made it impossible for me to do the thing I wanted to do, the thing I'd been waiting so long to do."

150

"Other people were also to blame," she persisted. "You can't . . . Blame me for part of it, if you will. I . . . "

"That's not very smart," he said, a half smile coming as he looked down at her. "I'm not blaming you for anything. We're partners, remember?"

She refused to meet his eyes then and he nodded quickly to Smith. "Take care of our partner, Mac. I'll be back."

He reached down to pull her hand away from the horse's bridle, squeezing the taut fingers just a little before pulling back. Then he whirled the horse and swung into the street, the big Springfield across his lap.

He rode hard for about twenty minutes but then let the horse set an easier pace. He didn't have to hurry. Trappe would scarcely be expecting such prompt pursuit. It would be just as well to let the precious trio get out of the hill country where he could stalk them at long range. Out in the open the big rifle would give him something of an advantage. This time he would have no qualms about taking whatever bulge circumstance might offer.

19

THE long downgrade made for easy travel but there was no ease in Kendrick's mind. Maybe Jo was right. Revenge was poor stuff, not worthy of a man who had claimed that his only object was to work his land in peace. Gunning down Amos Trappe wouldn't help Uncle Bill.

But there was more to it than that, he told himself angrily. No soldier worth his salt would stand siege and then let the enemy walk away with a victory and loot just when the defense was in a position to strike a telling counter blow. Trappe had a lot coming to him. It was time he got some of it.

The trail followed Packsaddle Creek for a good five miles but then cut through rugged country to avoid a long loop of the stream. After that there were a series of open flats and another rocky strip before the junction of the creek with the main Canadian River. It was on the second of these flats that Kendrick saw the three riders ahead. They were just entering one of the brushy strips but he was sure of them—and reasonably certain that they had not seen him on their back trail. Three miles ahead, he guessed. He was gaining rapidly. Maybe in the next open stretch he could get within rifle range. Then the advantage would be his.

He sent the horse across the open country at a good pace, slowing only when he entered the tangle of rocks and mesquite. From the look of the trail he judged that they had not even halted to look behind them. That brought a quick satisfaction and he spurred the horse again.

The haste almost made him miss the plain sign on the trail and he pulled up in quick alarm, sliding from the saddle and pulling his six-gun in one fluid motion. Something had happened here; the outlaws had halted.

"Getting careless, Kendrick," he told himself. A smart man didn't make that kind of mistakes. Unless he was lucky he didn't make them more than once. Then he shrugged and studied the sign. So he'd been lucky. It was about time.

The hoof marks in the trail were all mixed up as though three horses had gone into some kind of frenzied waltz before striking out southward from the trail. The sign showed the three men riding suspiciously close together and within the first twenty feet he found two blobs of fresh blood.

Watchful against an ambush he followed the sign, leading his horse as he tried to remain alert to several possibilities. Then he knew that he had wasted the precaution. The man in the mesquite clump was quite dead —and completely alone. It was Amos Trappe, the back of his fine broadcloth coat showing a jagged rent in the middle of a broad bloody patch.

It was easy to interpret the trail sign now. Trappe's men had doublecrossed him. One had probably pulled a gun on him while the other closed in from the rear to stab him between the shoulders. Then they had held the

152

body in the saddle long enough to haul it back away from the trail.

Kendrick didn't blame them very much. Trappe's insistence on burying one of his own men as a rustler must have given them something to think about. They must have realized that neither of them could expect better treatment. Fearful that he would betray them, they had simply beaten him to it. In the mind of the hired killers there couldn't have been much choice between risking the future treachery of Amos Trappe and claiming his loot for themselves.

A quick examination made it clear that Trappe was indeed dead, his pockets empty except for the original of the paper that had been left in the office, a paper which could mean nothing to the killers. Kendrick put it in his own pocket and climbed back into the saddle. Somehow he felt a little easier now. He still had a job to do but he didn't have to feel that he was doing it purely for revenge.

He forced the pace a little, knowing that the big valley could not be far ahead. Once out in the open Uncle Bill's rifle would be the key weapon. By outranging the fugitives he might even force them to abandon their loot in exchange for their lives. That would be enough. There had been too much of this killing already.

That was when he strained his luck for the second time. Suddenly a gun slammed and he could feel his horse going down. He managed to jump clear, running a few steps to save himself a fall and at the same time trying to see what had happened. Three more slugs whined past him and then he dove headlong into the cover of a juniper, still hanging onto the rifle.

Two more shots sounded, the bullets ticking brush above his head, but he made no move until he had the rifle ready and his hands steady. Evidently Spike and Haney had pulled off from the trail but had laid their ambush a little too far back for easy six-gun range. That was what had saved his hide; the bushwhack bullet intended for him had killed his horse.

He wiggled a little to one side in order to see better and was astonished to see Haney running straight toward

153

him. Maybe the man thought the quarry had gone down with a bullet or maybe he was just bold. Kendrick didn't bother to puzzle about it; he raised the rifle muzzle just as Haney let out a yell and started to blast with the six-gun. At that range it was cold turkey but Kendrick had no scruples now. This was how it had to be.

He saw Haney collapse in the middle of a stride but then he was trying to get around to meet the attack of the other man. Spike was driving in from another angle and Kendrick suddenly was all tangled up. He managed to eject the spent shell but when he reached for a fresh one he hit the wrong pocket. Before he could roll over to fumble on the other side a slug from the outlaw's gun struck the butt of the rifle. Kendrick knew that his left hand and wrist had gone numb but he didn't know whether he had been struck by the glancing bullet or whether it was simply shock. All he could do was to roll desperately, dragging at his Colt.

Another bullet burned the side of his neck but then the single-action was in his fist and he was lining his sights on the charging killer. The two guns exploded almost in unison but Kendrick's shot was just enough ahead so that he knocked Spike off balance. The outlaw's charge became a sprawling dive and when he slid to a halt he was not ten feet away, menacingly ugly but dead.

Kendrick climbed to his feet gingerly, dabbing at the trickle of blood that was beginning to run down into his shirt collar. The sound of racing hoofs came to him through the half daze which had succeeded the fight and he moved to take cover again, this time getting rifle ammunition where he could reach it.

A minute or so later he knew that the precaution was not necessary. Craddock and three other men were coming up out of the valley. This would be the law, he knew. It explained why Spike and Haney had gone into hiding. They hadn't intended to ambush him, probably because they didn't suspect he was on their trail. They had simply tried to dodge the approaching lawmen and had let themselves get caught between two parties. Their vicious attack had been simply an attempt to escape.

It was mid-afternoon when Kendrick returned to Pack-saddle with Craddock, Marshal Faulkner and the two deputies. There were three bodies on two led horses, Kendrick astride of the mount that had belonged to Amos Trappe. His own horse was dead in the scrub cedar country.

A crowd gathered quickly as they turned in at the trading post stables and it seemed evident that Mr. Glass had recovered sufficiently to take charge of business operations in the store. Mac winked approvingly as Kendrick dismounted, his expression hinting that he considered everything to be going quite well now that the last of the enemy had been so completely accounted for.

Kendrick was more concerned with the tight little frown on Jo's lips. She was worried, unhappy, and he thought he knew why. "Trappe got it from his own bully-boys," he told her as he came toward the side door of the post. "Then the killers ran out of luck and got caught between the law and me."

"Your neck?" she asked. "Are you hurt badly?"

He put his hand to the thin bandage that had been wrapped around his throat. "I plumb forgot about it," he confessed. "It's hardly even a nick. I'm getting a lot luckier lately."

"Will there be trouble over this shooting?" she asked. "With the law, I mean?"

"Not the way the marshal tells it. It seems that this man Craddock isn't as gullible as he looked. He smelt a rat when he saw how those NA men had been killed. So he asked for a real investigation instead of just making a report like he said he was going to do. He also asked a lot of questions about Trappe's business dealings. It looks like Amos played a real smart game—with two strings out. If he could get Spanish Ridge he would hold on here for all the outfit was worth. If anything went too far wrong—as it did—he was ready to pull out and leave your father holding the bag. The trading post is mort-gaged and practically none of the stock is paid for. Amos had everything in cash, ready to make tracks."

He handed her the paper he had taken from Trappe's pocket. "This is not legal, of course, but you'd better dis-

155

pose of it—along with the copy. The law probably won't make any fuss about your father taking over as the surviving partner but there's no point in raising questions. Now that he'll have the cash to run things he ought to be able to make something of the place. It might even turn out to be a good stand when we start hauling timber out."

Glass came to stand—a bit unsteadily—beside his daughter, hearing most of the statement. "I'm very grateful, sir," he said with forced dignity. "I fear that though I have deserved nothing I now stand to be a considerable gainer by virtue of the work of others, notably yourself."

Mac chuckled aloud as Kendrick shrugged. Kendrick said simply, "A lot of good business is largely luck, so think nothing of it."

Smith added, " 'Fortune brings in many boats that are not steered.' *Cymbeline*."

Kendrick joined in the somewhat nervous laugh but suggested, "You'd better move your assay office over here. With two jobs to keep you busy you might be better off."

"We've already arranged it," Jo said quietly. "When Father saw what he had signed while he was drunk he was willing to arrange things as I suggested. From here on he is owner—if the law permits it—but all management of the place is out of his hands."

"You propose to run things?"

"No. I decided that Mr. Smith would make a much better store manager than he would a hoeman. He agreed."

"Stole my partner, did you?"

She looked at him squarely for just a moment but then turned her eyes away with a flush coming to her cheeks. "I think that will work out well enough," she said quietly. Then she went back into the store and Kendrick could do nothing except exchange grins with the still-tipsy Mr. Glass.

That afternoon and evening Marshal Faulkner took voluminous testimony on every angle of the affair. With no coroner or other law in this part of the hills it seemed like a good idea to tie up everything as tightly as pos-

ble. There seemed to be no problem about having Glass
take over the partnership property but with the Kendrick
mix-up looming so large in the recent history of the valley
would be well to get everything down on paper.

The pieces fitted into place neatly enough. Glass was
undisputed owner of the Trappe enterprises, his ownership subject to Trappe's debts. North American would
lay a claim against the company for Trappe's actions in
helping to steal NA stock but Craddock assured them that
he would be happy to settle for a nominal sum, mostly to
show his stockholders that he was on the job.

Kendrick was, of course, the recognized owner of the
double homestead as well as Spanish Ridge. He and
Craddock completed an agreement between them where-
by the homestead lands would be used only in part for
market crops. NA needed winter hay and Kendrick would
undertake to supply it from the hay lands along the creek.
And NA would retain a right-of-way for cattle drives
across the Kendrick property. With a deal like that there
should be no reason for any clash of interest between
cattleman and homesteader.

"I think we're pretty well squared away," Kendrick
told Smith when they found a chance to get away from
the rush of arrangements. "You told me in the beginning
you were no farmer so I imagine you're satisfied."

"Better than I could have hoped. My biggest problem
will be to keep the boss out of the bar but I think I know
now to handle that."

"How?"

"Back on the Mississippi we set out to cure a man of
his drinking habits and it was real easy when we found
out about some stuff we could put in his liquor. It won't
show up in the taste, but it sure makes a fellow sick. I'll
get me a supply and tell the bartender that some of it
goes into every drink Glass takes—after the first one."

He winked and struck a pose. "Poison be their drink!
Gall, worse than gall, the daintiest that they taste."

"Is that a real one or did you make it up?"

"Henry the Sixth. Honest."

Kendrick laughed. "I believe you."

Jo came in then, a thin smile breaking through as she

caught a hint of the good humor between the two men. "It sounds as though you might have gotten everything fixed up to your complete satisfaction."

"Almost," Mac told her. "When we get Michaels broken in as livery stable boss we'll have everybody accounted for but you."

"Don't worry about me," she retorted. "I can . . . '

"You're frowning," Mac interrupted. "There's no call to be sad just because some worthless polecats got what was coming to them. On our side we're due to celebrate."

She stared at him quizzically. "Me celebrate? Mister, I've got saddle blisters!"

The remaining tension exploded in a roar of laughter, Jo joining in even as she protested, "It's not funny!"

"Then I'll be serious," Mac told her, resuming his mock gravity. "There's a business matter to complete. A little while ago we formed a partnership. Now I'm otherwise engaged. I now call for the dissolution of that partnership. Anyone opposed?"

He did not wait for a reply but went on quickly. "Now I propose that the two of you form a new partnership to replace the dissolved one. It's a natural thing to do. Both of you like that dirt-farming business and both of you seem to have a hankering for the particular bit of dirt up the creek. For Tom it would be real convenient to have a partner who knows the business so well. For you, Mrs. Kendrick, it would save you the trouble of getting used to a new name."

The girl seemed to be having trouble in finding words so Kendrick broke in with a perfectly straight face. "I can quote some Shakespeare at this point. From *Merry Wives of Windsor,* I think. 'But if you say "Marry her" I will marry her'. That's an offer."

"You keep out of this!" Smith ordered. "You had your chance to make that offer some time ago. You didn't do it. Now I'm running the show."

Kendrick grinned meekly. "I didn't think the lady was ready for a proposition."

"A lady is always ready for a proposition," Smith stated firmly. "And another thing . . . stop stealing my act with the Shakespeare stuff!"

"Yes, sir." Still very meek.

"It figures like this," Smith went on in the same brisk manner. "I want to see this new partnership squared away. There's an honest clerk at Cimarron who wants it fixed up the same way. That makes two of us. Suppose the pair of you wander outside and see if you can't rustle up a couple more votes for a good cause."

Kendrick stole a sideways glance at the girl and caught just a trace of a wink. Her voice was steady, almost solemn, however, as she nodded to Smith. "We'll discuss it," she agreed. "But please remember that there are a great many things to be said against it."

"Name one!"

"Very well, if you insist. I'm practically a nameless widow with a background of fraud. I don't . . . "

Kendrick took her arm and steered her toward the door. "Come along—partner. I'm not figuring to quote Shakespeare now." He turned to wink at Mac as they went out. "You can count on those other two votes. And stop smirking; we're going out to talk business!"

Ride into the world of adventure with Ballantine's western novels!